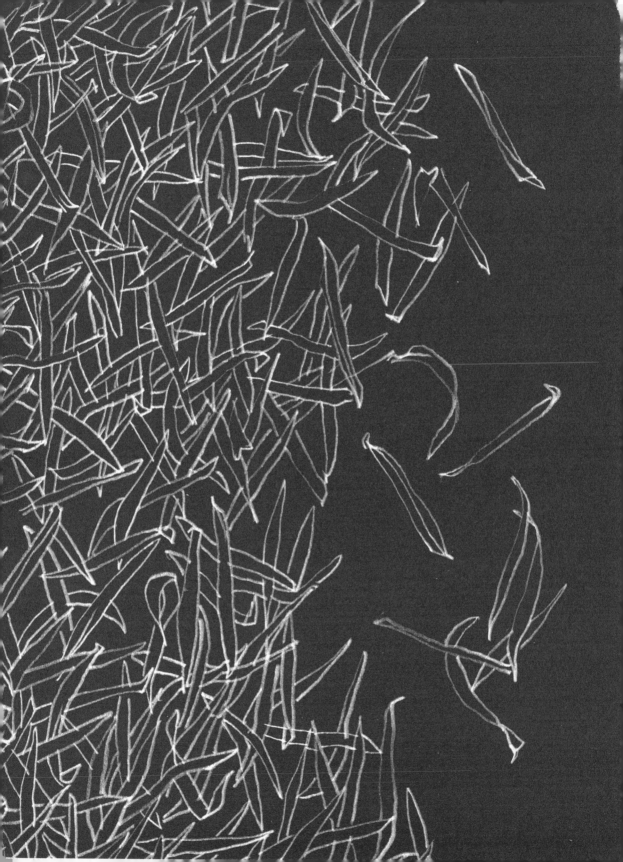

A MONSTER CALLS

Special Collectors' Edition

WITHDRAWN

A MONSTER CALLS

SPECIAL COLLECTORS' EDITION

A novel by **Patrick Ness**

Inspired by an idea from **Siobhan Dowd**

Illustrations by **Jim Kay**

With additional material from

J.A. Bayona, Liam Neeson, Sigourney Weaver,

Felicity Jones, *and* **Lewis MacDougall**

CANDLEWICK PRESS

CONTENTS

A MONSTER CALLS

AUTHORS' NOTE

I never got to meet Siobhan Dowd. I only know her the way that most of the rest of you will–through her superb books. Four electric young adult novels, two published in her lifetime, two after her too-early death. If you haven't read them, remedy that oversight immediately.

This would have been her fifth book. She had the characters, a premise, and a beginning. What she didn't have, unfortunately, was time.

When I was asked if I would consider turning her work into a book, I hesitated. What I wouldn't do–what I *couldn't* do– was write a novel mimicking her voice. That would have been a disservice to her, to the reader, and most importantly to the story. I don't think good writing can possibly work that way.

But the thing about good ideas is that they grow other ideas. Almost before I could help it, Siobhan's ideas were suggesting new ones to me, and I began to feel that itch that every writer longs for: the itch to start getting words down, the itch to tell a story.

I felt–and feel–as if I've been handed a baton, like a particularly fine writer has given me her story and said, "Go. Run with it. Make trouble." So that's what I tried to do. Along the way,

I had only a single guideline: to write a book I think Siobhan would have liked. No other criteria could really matter.

And now it's time to hand the baton on to you. Stories don't end with the writers, however many started the race. Here's what Siobhan and I came up with. So go. Run with it.

Make trouble.

Patrick Ness
London, February 2011

FOR SIOBHAN

You're only young once, they say, but doesn't it go on for a long time? More years than you can bear.

Hilary Mantel, *An Experiment in Love*

A MONSTER CALLS

The monster showed up just after midnight. As they do.

Conor was awake when it came.

He'd had a nightmare. Well, not *a* nightmare. *The* nightmare. The one he'd been having a lot lately. The one with the darkness and the wind and the screaming. The one with the hands slipping from his grasp, no matter how hard he tried to hold on. The one that always ended with–

"Go away," Conor whispered into the darkness of his bedroom, trying to push the nightmare back, not let it follow him into the world of waking. "Go away now."

He glanced over at the clock his mum had put on his bedside table. 12:07. Seven minutes past midnight. Which was late for a school night, late for a Sunday, certainly.

He'd told no one about the nightmare. Not his mum, obviously, but no one else either, not his dad in their fortnightly (or so) phone call, *definitely* not his grandma, and no one at school. Absolutely not.

I

What happened in the nightmare was something no one else ever needed to know.

Conor blinked groggily at his room, then he frowned. There was something he was missing. He sat up in his bed, waking a bit more. The nightmare was slipping from him, but there was something he couldn't put his finger on, something different, something–

He listened, straining against the silence, but all he could hear was the quiet house around him, the occasional tick from the empty downstairs or a rustle of bedding from his mum's room next door.

Nothing.

And then something. Something he realized was the thing that had woken him.

Someone was calling his name.

Conor.

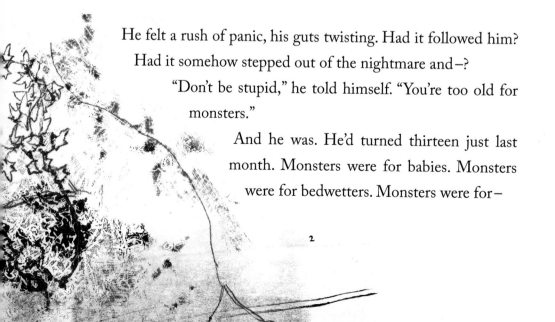

He felt a rush of panic, his guts twisting. Had it followed him? Had it somehow stepped out of the nightmare and–?

"Don't be stupid," he told himself. "You're too old for monsters."

And he was. He'd turned thirteen just last month. Monsters were for babies. Monsters were for bedwetters. Monsters were for–

Conor.

There it was again. Conor swallowed. It had been an unusually warm October, and his window was still open. Maybe the curtains shushing each other in the small breeze could have sounded like –

Conor.

All right, it wasn't the wind. It was definitely a voice, but not one he recognized. It wasn't his mother's, that was for sure. It wasn't a woman's voice at all, and he wondered for a crazy moment if his dad had somehow made a surprise trip from America and arrived too late to phone and –

Conor.

No. Not his dad. This voice had a quality to it, a *monstrous* quality, wild and untamed.

Then he heard a heavy creak of wood outside, as if something gigantic was stepping across a timber floor.

He didn't want to go and look. But at the same time, a part of him wanted to look more than anything.

Wide awake now, he pushed back the covers, got out of bed, and went over to the window. In the pale half-light of the moon, he could clearly see the church tower up on the small hill behind his house, the one with the train tracks curving beside it, two hard steel lines glowing dully in the night. The moon shone, too, on the graveyard attached to the church, filled with tombstones you could hardly read anymore.

Conor could also see the great yew tree that rose from the center of the graveyard, a tree so ancient it almost seemed to be made of the same stone as the church. He only knew it was a yew because his mother had told him, first when he was little to make sure he didn't eat the berries, which were poisonous, and again this past year, when she'd started staring out of their kitchen window with a funny look on her face and saying, "That's a yew tree, you know."

And then he heard his name again.

Conor.

Like it was being whispered in both his ears.

"What?" Conor said, his heart thumping, suddenly impatient for whatever was going to happen.

A cloud moved in front of the moon, covering the whole landscape in darkness, and a *whoosh* of wind rushed down the hill and into his room, billowing the curtains. He heard the creaking and cracking of wood again, groaning like a living thing, like the hungry stomach of the world growling for a meal.

Then the cloud passed, and the moon shone again.

On the yew tree.

Which now stood firmly in the middle of his backyard.

And here was the monster.

As Conor watched, the uppermost branches of the tree gathered themselves into a great and terrible face, shimmering

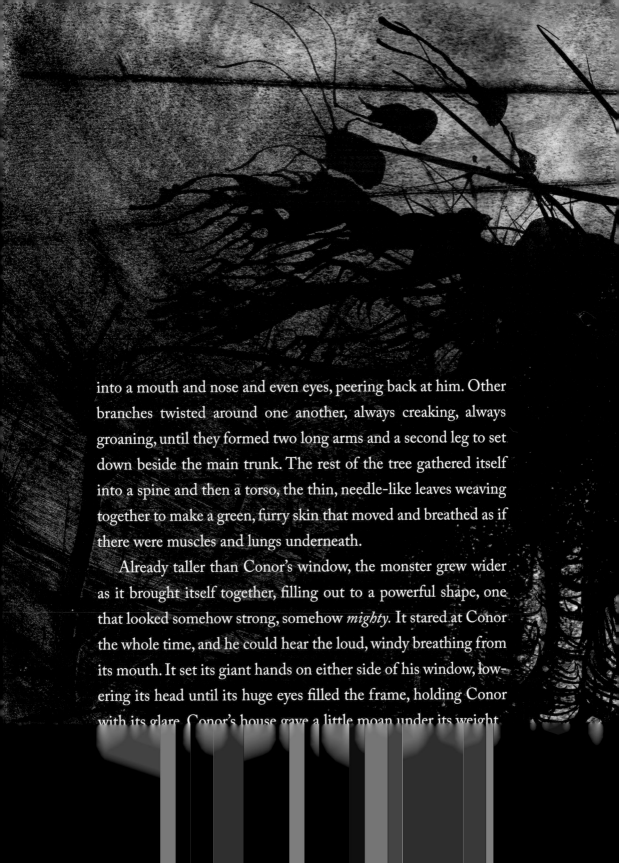

into a mouth and nose and even eyes, peering back at him. Other branches twisted around one another, always creaking, always groaning, until they formed two long arms and a second leg to set down beside the main trunk. The rest of the tree gathered itself into a spine and then a torso, the thin, needle-like leaves weaving together to make a green, furry skin that moved and breathed as if there were muscles and lungs underneath.

Already taller than Conor's window, the monster grew wider as it brought itself together, filling out to a powerful shape, one that looked somehow strong, somehow *mighty*. It stared at Conor the whole time, and he could hear the loud, windy breathing from its mouth. It set its giant hands on either side of his window, lowering its head until its huge eyes filled the frame, holding Conor with its glare. Conor's house gave a little moan under its weight.

And then the monster spoke.

Conor O'Malley, it said, a huge gust of warm, compost-smelling breath rushing through Conor's window, blowing his hair back. Its voice rumbled low and loud, with a vibration so deep Conor could feel it in his chest.

I have come to get you, Conor O'Malley, the monster said, pushing against the house, shaking the pictures off Conor's wall, sending books and electronic gadgets and an old stuffed toy rhino tumbling to the floor.

A monster, Conor thought. A real, honest-to-goodness monster. In real, waking life. Not in a dream, but here, at his window.

Come to get him.

But Conor didn't run.

In fact, he found he wasn't even frightened.

All he could feel, all he *had* felt since the monster revealed itself, was a growing disappointment.

Because this wasn't the monster he was expecting.

"So come and get me then," he said.

A strange quiet fell.

What did you say? the monster asked.

Conor crossed his arms. "I said, come and get me then."

The monster paused for a moment, and then with a *roar* it pounded two fists against the house. Conor's ceiling buckled under the blows, and huge cracks appeared in the walls. Wind filled the room, the air thundering with the monster's angry bellows.

"Shout all you want," Conor shrugged, barely raising his voice. "I've seen worse."

The monster roared even louder and smashed an arm through Conor's window, shattering glass and wood and brick. A huge, twisted, branch-wound hand grabbed Conor around the middle and lifted him off the floor. It swung him out of his room and into the night, high above his backyard, holding him up against the circle of the moon, its fingers clenching so hard against Conor's ribs he could barely breathe. Conor could see raggedy teeth made of hard, knotted wood in the monster's open mouth, and he felt warm breath rushing up toward him.

Then the monster paused again.

You really aren't afraid, are you?

"No," Conor said. "Not of you, anyway."

The monster narrowed its eyes.

You will be, it said. *Before the end.*

And the last thing Conor remembered was the monster's mouth roaring open to eat him alive.

BREAKFAST

"Mum?" Conor asked, stepping into the kitchen. He knew she wouldn't be in there—he couldn't hear the kettle boiling, which she always did first thing—but he'd found himself asking for her a lot lately when he entered rooms in the house. He didn't want to startle her, just in case she'd fallen asleep somewhere she hadn't planned to.

But she wasn't in the kitchen. Which meant she was probably still up in her bed. Which meant Conor would have to make his own breakfast, something he'd grown used to doing. Fine. *Good*, in fact, especially *this* morning.

He walked quickly to the trash and stuffed the plastic bag he was carrying down near the bottom, covering it up with other rubbish so it wouldn't be obvious.

"There," he said to no one, and stood breathing for a second. Then he nodded to himself and said, "Breakfast."

Some bread in the toaster, some cereal in a bowl, some juice in a glass, and he was ready to go, sitting down at the little table in the kitchen to eat. His mum had her own bread and cereal which she bought at a health-food shop in town and which Conor

thankfully didn't have to share. It tasted as unhappy as it looked.

He looked up at the clock. Twenty-five minutes before he had to leave. He was already in his school uniform, his rucksack packed for the day and waiting by the front door. All things he'd done for himself.

He sat with his back to the kitchen window, the one over the sink that looked out onto their small backyard, across the train tracks and up to the church with its graveyard.

And its yew tree.

Conor took another bite of his cereal. His chewing was the only sound in the whole house.

It had been a dream. What else *could* it have been?

When he'd opened his eyes this morning, the first thing he'd looked at was his window. It had still been there, of course, no damage at all, no gaping hole into the yard. Of *course* it had. Only a baby would have thought it really happened. Only a baby would believe that a tree–seriously, a *tree*–had walked down the hill and attacked the house.

He'd laughed a little at the thought, at how stupid it all was, and he'd stepped out of bed.

To the sound of a crunch beneath his feet.

Every inch of his bedroom floor was covered in short, spiky yew tree leaves.

He put another bite of cereal in his mouth, definitely not looking at the rubbish bin, where he had stuffed the plastic bag full of leaves he'd swept up this morning first thing.

It had been a windy night. They'd clearly blown in through his open window.

Clearly.

He finished his cereal and toast, drank the last of his juice, then rinsed the dishes and put them in the dishwasher. Still twenty minutes to go. He decided to empty the rubbish bin altogether – less risky that way – and took the bag out to the wheelie bin in front of the house. Since he was already making the trip, he gathered up the recycling and put that out, too. Then he got a load of sheets going in the washer that he'd hang out on the line when he got home from school.

He went back to the kitchen and looked at the clock.

Still ten minutes left.

Still no sign of –

"Conor?" he heard, from the top of the stairs.

He let out a long breath he hadn't realized he was holding in.

"You've had breakfast?" his mum asked, leaning against the kitchen doorframe.

"Yes, Mum," Conor said, rucksack in his hand.

"You're sure?"

"*Yes*, Mum."

She looked at him doubtfully. Conor rolled his eyes. "Toast and cereal and juice," he said. "I put the dishes in the dishwasher."

"And took the rubbish out," his mum said quietly, looking at how neat he'd left the kitchen.

"There's washing going, too," Conor said.

"You're a good boy," she said, and though she was smiling, he could hear sadness in it, too. "I'm sorry I wasn't up."

"It's okay."

"It's just this new round of–"

"It's *okay*," Conor said.

She stopped, but she still smiled back at him. She hadn't tied her scarf around her head yet this morning, and her bare scalp looked too soft, too fragile in the morning light, like a baby's. It made Conor's stomach hurt to see it.

"Was that you I heard last night?" she asked.

Conor froze. "When?"

"Sometime after midnight, must have been," she said, shuffling over to switch on the kettle. "I thought I was dreaming but I could have sworn I heard your voice."

"Probably just talking in my sleep," Conor said, flatly.

"Probably," his mum yawned. She took a mug off the rack hanging by the fridge. "I forgot to tell you," she said, lightly, "your grandma's coming by tomorrow."

Conor's shoulders sank. "Aw, *Mum.*"

"I know," she said, "but you shouldn't have to make your own breakfast every morning."

"*Every* morning?" Conor said. "How long is she going to be here?"

"Conor—"

"We don't need her here—"

"You know how I get at this point in the treatments, Conor—"

"We've been okay so far—"

"*Conor,*" his mum snapped, so harshly it seemed to surprise them both. There was a long silence. And then she smiled again, looking really, really tired.

"I'll try to keep it as short as possible, okay?" she said. "I know you don't like giving up your room, and I'm sorry. I wouldn't have asked her if I didn't need her to come, all right?"

Conor had to sleep on the settee every time his grandmother came to stay. But that wasn't it. He didn't like the way she *talked* to him, like he was an employee under evaluation. An evaluation he was going to fail. Plus, they *had* always managed so far, just the two of them, no matter how bad the treatments made her feel, it was the price she paid to get better, so why–?

"Only a couple of nights," his mum said, as if she could read his mind. "Don't worry, okay?"

He picked at the zipper on his rucksack, not saying anything, trying to think of other things. And then he remembered the bag of leaves he'd stuffed into the rubbish bin.

Maybe grandma staying in his room wasn't the worst thing that could happen.

"There's the smile I love," his mum said, reaching for the kettle as it clicked off. Then she said, with mock-horror, "She's going to bring me some of her old *wigs*, if you can believe it." She rubbed her bare head with her free hand. "I'll look like a zombie Margaret Thatcher."

"I'm going to be late," Conor said, eyeing the clock.

"Okay, sweetheart," she said, teetering over to kiss him on the forehead. "You're a good boy," she said again. "I wish you didn't have to be quite *so* good."

As he left to head off for school, he saw her take her tea over to the kitchen window above the sink, and when he opened the front door to leave, he heard her say, "There's that old yew tree," as if she was talking to herself.

SCHOOL

He could already taste the blood in his mouth as he got up. He had bitten the inside of his lip when he hit the ground, and it was what he focused on now as he stood, the strange metallic flavor that made you want to spit it out immediately, like you'd eaten something that wasn't food at all.

He swallowed it instead. Harry and his cronies would have been thrilled beyond words if they knew Conor was bleeding. He could hear Anton and Sully laughing behind him, knew exactly the look on Harry's face, even though he couldn't see it. He could probably even guess what Harry would say next in that calm, amused voice of his that seemed to mimic every adult you never wanted to meet.

"Be careful of the steps there," Harry said. "You might fall."

Yep, that'd be about right.

It hadn't always been like this.

Harry was the Blond Wonder Child, the teachers' pet through every year of school. The first pupil with his hand in the air, the fastest player on the soccer field, but for all that, just another kid in Conor's class. They hadn't been friends exactly–Harry didn't really have friends, only followers; Anton and Sully basically just stood behind him and laughed at everything he did–but they hadn't been enemies, either. Conor would have been mildly surprised if Harry had even known his name.

Somewhere over the past year, though, something had changed. Harry had started noticing Conor, catching his eye, looking at him with a detached amusement.

This change hadn't come when everything started with Conor's mum. No, it had come later, when Conor started having the nightmare, the *real* nightmare, not the stupid tree, the nightmare with the screaming and the falling, the nightmare he would never tell another living soul about. When Conor started having *that* nightmare, that's when Harry noticed him, like a secret mark had been placed on him that only Harry could see.

A mark that drew Harry to him like iron to a magnet.

On the first day of the new school year, Harry had tripped Conor coming into the school grounds, sending him tumbling to the pavement.

And so it had begun.

And so it had continued.

—— · ——

Conor kept his back turned as Anton and Sully laughed. He ran his tongue along the inside of his lip to see how bad the bite was. Not terrible. He'd live, if he could make it to class without anything further happening.

But then something further happened.

"Leave him alone!" Conor heard, wincing at the sound.

He turned and saw Lily Andrews pushing her furious face into Harry's, which only made Anton and Sully laugh even harder.

"Your poodle's here to save you," Anton said.

"I'm just making it a fair fight," Lily huffed, her wiry curls bouncing around all poodle-like, no matter how tightly she'd tied them back.

"You're bleeding, O'Malley," Harry said, calmly ignoring Lily.

Conor put his hand up to his mouth too late to catch a bit of blood coming out of the corner.

"He'll have to get his baldy mother to kiss it better for him!" Sully crowed.

Conor's stomach contracted to a ball of fire, like a little sun burning him up from the inside, but before he could react, Lily did. With a cry of outrage, she pushed an astonished Sully into the shrubbery, toppling him all the way over.

"Lillian Andrews!" came the voice of doom from halfway across the yard.

They froze. Even Sully paused in the act of getting up.

Miss Kwan, their Head of Year, was storming over to them, her scariest frown burnt into her face like a scar.

"They started it, Miss," Lily said, already defending herself.

"I don't want to hear it," Miss Kwan said. "Are you all right, Sullivan?"

Sully shot a quick glance at Lily, then got a pained look across his face. "I don't know, Miss," he said. "I might need to go home."

"Don't milk it," Miss Kwan said. "To my office, Lillian."

"But Miss, they were—"

"*Now*, Lillian."

"They were making fun of Conor's mother!"

This made everyone freeze again, and the burning sun in Conor's stomach grew hotter, ready to eat him alive.

(—and in his mind, he felt a flash of the nightmare, of the howling wind, of the burning blackness—)

He pushed it away.

"Is this true, Conor?" Miss Kwan asked, her face as serious as a sermon.

The blood on Conor's tongue made him want to throw up. He looked over to Harry and his cronies. Anton and Sully seemed worried, but Harry just stared back at him, unruffled and calm, like he was genuinely curious as to what Conor might say.

"No, Miss, it's not true," Conor said, swallowing the blood. "I just fell. They were helping me up."

Lily's face turned instantly into hurt surprise. Her mouth dropped open, but she made no sound.

"Get to your classes," Miss Kwan said. "Except for you, Lillian."

Lily kept looking back at Conor as Miss Kwan pulled her away, but Conor turned from her.

To find Harry holding his rucksack out for him.

"Well done, O'Malley," Harry said.

Conor said nothing, just took the bag from him roughly and made his way inside.

LIFE WRITING

Stories, Conor thought with dread as he walked home.

It was after school, and he'd made his escape. He'd gotten through the rest of the day avoiding Harry and the others, though they probably knew better than to risk causing him another "accident" so soon after nearly getting caught by Miss Kwan. He'd also avoided Lily, who had returned to lessons with red, puffy eyes and a scowl you could hang meat from. When the final bell rang, Conor had rushed out fast, feeling the burden of school and of Harry and of Lily drop from his shoulders as he put one street and then another between himself and all of that.

Stories, he thought again.

"*Your* stories," Mrs. Marl had said in their English lesson. "Don't think you haven't lived long enough to have a story to tell."

Life writing, she'd called it, an assignment for them to write about themselves. Their family tree, where they'd lived, holiday trips, and happy memories.

Important things that had happened.

Conor shifted his rucksack on his shoulder. He could think of a couple of important things that had happened. Nothing he wanted to write about, though. His father leaving. The cat wandering off one day and never coming back.

The afternoon when his mother said they needed to have a little talk.

He frowned and kept walking.

But then again, he also remembered the day *before* that day. His mum had taken him to his favorite Indian restaurant and let him order as much vindaloo as he wanted. Then she'd laughed and said, "Why the hell not?" and ordered plates of it for herself, too. They'd started farting before they'd even got back in the car. On the drive home, they could hardly talk from laughing and farting so hard.

Conor smiled just thinking about it. Because it *hadn't* been a drive home. It had been a surprise trip to the cinema on a school night, to a film Conor had already seen four times but knew his mum was sick to death of. There they were, though, sitting through it again, still giggling to themselves, eating buckets of popcorn and drinking buckets of Coke.

Conor wasn't stupid. When they'd had the "little talk" the next day, he knew what his mum had done and why she had done it. But that didn't take away from how much fun that night had been. How hard they'd laughed. How anything had seemed possible. How anything good could have happened to them right then and there and they wouldn't have been surprised.

But he wasn't going to be writing about *that* either.

"Hey!" A voice calling behind him made him groan. "Hey, Conor, wait!"

Lily.

"Hey!" she said, catching up with him and planting herself right in his way so he had to stop or run into her. She was out of breath, but her face was still furious. "Why did you do that today?" she said.

"Leave me alone," Conor said, pushing past her.

"Why didn't you tell Miss Kwan what really happened?" Lily persisted, following him. "Why did you let me get into trouble?"

"Why did you butt in when it was none of your business?"

"I was trying to *help* you."

"I don't need your help," Conor said. "I was doing fine on my own."

"You were not!" Lily said. "You were bleeding."

"It's none of your *business*," Conor snapped again and picked up his pace.

"I've got detention *all week*," Lily complained. "*And* a note home to my parents."

"That's not my problem."

"But it's your fault."

Conor stopped suddenly and turned to her. He looked so angry she stepped back, startled, almost like she was afraid. "It's *your* fault," he said. "It's *all* your fault."

He stormed off back down the pavement. "We used to be friends," Lily called after him.

"*Used* to be," Conor said without turning around.

He'd known Lily forever. Or for as long as he could remember, which was basically the same thing.

Their mums were friends from before Conor and Lily were born, and Lily had been like a sister who lived in another house, especially when one mum or the other would babysit. He and Lily had only been friends, though, none of the romantic stuff they got teased for sometimes at school. In a way, it was hard for Conor to even look at Lily as a *girl*, at least not in the same way as the other girls at school. How could you when you'd both played sheep in the same nativity play, aged five? When you knew how much she used to pick her nose? When *she* knew how long you'd needed a night-light after your father moved out? It had just been a friendship, normal as anything.

But then his mum's "little talk" had happened, and what came next was simple, really, and sudden.

No one knew.

Then Lily's mum knew, of course.

Then Lily knew.

And then everyone knew. Everyone. Which changed the whole world in a single day.

And he was never going to forgive her for that.

Another street and another street more and there was his house, small but detached. It had been the one thing his mum had insisted on in the divorce, that it was theirs free and clear and they wouldn't have to move after his dad had left for America with Stephanie, the new wife. That had been six years ago, so long now that Conor sometimes couldn't remember what it was like having a dad in the house.

Didn't mean he still didn't think about it, though.

He looked up past his house to the hill beyond, the church steeple poking up into the cloudy sky.

And the yew tree hovering over the graveyard like a sleeping giant.

Conor forced himself to keep looking at it, making himself see that it was just a tree, a tree like any other, like any one of those that lined the railway track.

A tree. That's all it was. That's all it *ever* was. A tree.

A tree that, as he watched, reared up a giant face to look at him in the sunlight, its arms reaching out, its voice saying, *Conor—*

He stepped back so fast, he nearly fell into the street, catching himself on the hood of a parked car.

When he looked back up, it was just a tree again.

THREE STORIES

He lay in his bed that night, wide awake, watching the clock on his bedside table.

It had been the slowest evening imaginable. Cooking frozen lasagna had tired his mum out so badly she fell asleep five minutes into *EastEnders*. Conor hated the program but he made sure it recorded for her, then he spread a duvet over her and went and did the dishes.

His mum's mobile had gone off once, not waking her. Conor saw it was Lily's mum calling and let it go to voice mail. He did his schoolwork at the kitchen table, stopping before he got to Mrs. Marl's Life Writing homework, then he played around on the Internet for a while in his room before brushing his teeth and seeing himself to bed. He'd barely turned out the light when his mum had very apologetically—and very groggily—come in to kiss him good night.

A few minutes later, he'd heard her in the bathroom, throwing up.

"Do you need any help?" he'd called from his bed.

"No, sweetheart," his mum called back, weakly. "I'm kind of used to it by now."

That was the thing. Conor was used to it, too. It was always the second and third days after the treatments that were the worst, always the days when she was the most tired, when she threw up the most. It had almost become normal.

After a while, the throwing up had stopped. He'd heard the bathroom light click off and her bedroom door shut.

That was two hours ago. He'd lain awake since then, waiting.

But for what?

His bedside clock read 12:05. Then it read 12:06. He looked over to his bedroom window, shut tight even though the night was still warm. His clock ticked over to 12:07.

He got up, went over to the window, and looked out.

The monster stood in his yard, looking right back at him.

Open up, the monster said, its voice as clear as if the window wasn't between them. *I want to talk to you.*

"Yeah, sure," Conor said, keeping his voice low. "Because that's what monsters always want. To *talk.*"

The monster smiled. It was a ghastly sight. *If I must force my way in,* it said, *I will do so happily.*

It raised a gnarled woody fist to punch through the wall of Conor's bedroom.

"No!" Conor said. "I don't want you to wake my mum."

Then come outside, the monster said, and even in his room,

Conor's nose filled with the moist smell of earth and wood and sap.

"What do you want from me?" Conor said.

The monster pressed its face close to the window.

It is not what I want from you, Conor O'Malley, it said. *It is what **you** want from **me**.*

"I don't want anything from you," Conor said.

Not yet, said the monster. *But you will.*

"It's only a dream," Conor said to himself in the backyard, looking up at the monster silhouetted against the moon in the night sky. He folded his arms tightly against his body, not because it was cold, but because he couldn't actually believe he'd tiptoed down the stairs, unlocked the back door, and come outside.

He still felt calm. Which was weird. This nightmare—because it was surely a nightmare, of course it was—was so different from the other nightmare.

No terror, no panic, no darkness, for one thing.

And yet here was a monster, clear as the clearest night, towering thirty or forty feet above him, breathing heavily in the night air.

"It's only a dream," he said again.

But what is a dream, Conor O'Malley? the monster said, bending down so its face was close to Conor's. *Who is to say that it is not everything **else** that is the dream?*

Every time the monster moved, Conor could hear the creak of wood, groaning and yawning in the monster's huge body. He could see, too, the power in the monster's arms, great wiry ropes of branches constantly twisting and shifting together in what must have been tree muscle, connected to a massive trunk of a chest, topped by a head and teeth that could chomp him down in one bite.

"What are you?" Conor asked, pulling his arms closer around himself.

I am not a "what," frowned the monster. *I am a "who."*

"*Who* are you, then?" Conor said.

The monster's eyes widened. *Who am I?* it said, its voice getting louder. ***Who am I?***

The monster seemed to grow before Conor's eyes, getting taller and broader. A sudden, hard wind swirled up around them, and the monster spread its arms out wide, so wide they seemed to reach to opposite horizons, so wide they seemed big enough to encompass the world.

I have had as many names as there are years to time itself! roared the monster. *I am Herne the Hunter! I am Cernunnos! I am the eternal Green Man!*

A great arm swung down and snatched Conor up in it, lifting him high in the air, the wind whirling around them, making the monster's leafy skin wave angrily.

Who am I? the monster repeated, still roaring. *I am the spine that the mountains hang upon! I am the tears that the rivers cry! I am the lungs that breathe the wind! I am the wolf that kills the stag, the hawk that kills the mouse, the spider that kills the fly! I am the stag, the mouse, and the fly that are eaten! I am the snake of the world devouring its tail! I am everything untamed and untameable!* It brought Conor up close to its eye. *I am this wild earth, come for you, Conor O'Malley.*

"You look like a tree," Conor said.

The monster squeezed him until he cried out.

I do not often come walking, boy, the monster said, *only for matters of life and death. I expect to be listened to.*

The monster loosened its grip, and Conor could breathe again. "So what do you want with *me*?" Conor asked.

The monster gave an evil grin. The wind died down and a quiet fell. *At last*, said the monster. *To the matter at hand. The reason I have come walking.*

Conor tensed, suddenly dreading what was coming.

Here is what will happen, Conor O'Malley, the monster continued, *I will come to you again on further nights.*

Conor felt his stomach clench, like he was preparing for a blow.

And I will tell you three stories. Three tales from when I walked before.

Conor blinked. Then blinked again. "You're going to tell me *stories*?"

Indeed, the monster said.

"Well–" Conor looked around in disbelief. "How is *that* a nightmare?"

Stories are the wildest things of all, the monster rumbled. *Stories chase and bite and hunt.*

"That's what *teachers* always say," Conor said. "No one believes them either."

And when I have finished my three stories, the monster said, as if Conor hadn't spoken, *you will tell me a fourth.*

Conor squirmed in the monster's hand. "I'm no good at stories."

You will tell me a fourth, the monster repeated, *and it will be the truth.*

"The truth?"

Not just any truth. **Your** *truth.*

"O-*kay*," Conor said, "but you said I'd be scared before the end of all this, and that doesn't sound scary at all."

You know that is not true, the monster said. *You know that your truth, the one that you hide, Conor O'Malley, is the thing you are most afraid of.*

Conor stopped squirming.

It couldn't mean –

There was no *way* it could mean –

There was no way it could know *that.*

No. *No.* He was *never* going to say what happened in the real nightmare. Never in a million years.

You will tell it, the monster said. *For this is why you called me.*

Conor grew even more confused. "*Called* you? I didn't *call* you –"

You will tell me the fourth tale. You will tell me the truth.

"And what if I don't?" Conor said.

The monster gave the evil grin again. *Then I will eat you alive.*

And its mouth opened impossibly wide, wide enough to eat the whole world, wide enough to make Conor disappear forever—

He sat up in bed with a shout.

His bed. He was back in his bed.

Of course it was a dream. Of *course* it was. *Again.*

He sighed angrily and rubbed his eyes with the heels of his hands. How was he ever going to get any rest if his dreams were going to be this tiring?

He'd get himself a drink of water, he thought as he threw back the covers. He'd get up and he'd start this night over again, forgetting all this stupid dream business that made no sense whatso—

Something squished under his foot.

He switched on his lamp. His floor was covered in poisonous red yew tree berries.

Which had all somehow come in through a closed and locked window.

GRANDMA

"Are you being a good boy for your mum?"

Conor's grandma pinched Conor's cheeks so hard he swore she was going to draw blood.

"He's been *very* good, Ma," Conor's mother said, winking at him from behind his grandma, her favorite blue scarf tied around her head. "So there's no need to inflict quite so much pain."

"Oh, nonsense," his grandma said, giving him two playful slaps on each cheek that actually hurt quite a lot. "Why don't you go and put the kettle on for me and your mum?" she said, making it sound not like a question at all.

As Conor gratefully left the room, his grandma placed her hands on her hips and looked at his mother. "Now then, my dear," he heard her say as he went into the kitchen. "What *are* we going to do with you?"

Conor's grandma wasn't like other grandmas. He'd met Lily's grandma loads of times, and *she* was how grandmas were supposed to be: crinkly and smiley, with white hair and the whole lot. She cooked meals where she made three separate eternally boiled vegetable portions for everybody and would giggle in the corner at Christmas with a small glass of sherry and a paper crown on her head.

Conor's grandma wore tailored pantsuits, dyed her hair to keep out the gray, and said things that made no sense at all, like "Sixty is the new fifty" or "Classic cars need the most expensive polish." What did that even *mean*? She emailed birthday cards, would argue with waiters over wine, and still had a *job*. Her house was even worse, filled with expensive old things you could never touch, like a clock she wouldn't even let the cleaning lady dust. Which was another thing. What kind of grandma had a cleaning lady?

"Two sugars, no milk," she called from the sitting room as Conor made the tea. As if he didn't know that from the last three thousand times she'd visited.

"Thank you, my boy," his grandma said when he brought in the tea.

"Thank you, sweetheart," his mum said, smiling at him out of view of his grandma, still inviting him to join with her against her mother. He couldn't help himself. He smiled back a little.

"And how was school today, young man?" his grandma asked.

"Fine," Conor said.

It hadn't really been fine. Lily was still fuming, Harry had put a marker pen with its cap off deep in his rucksack, and Miss Kwan had pulled him aside to ask, with a serious look on her face, How He Was Holding Up.

"You know," his grandma said, setting down her cup of tea, "there's a tremendous independent boys' school not half a mile from my house. I've been looking into it, and the academic standards are quite high, much higher than he's getting at the comprehensive, I'm sure."

Conor stared at her. Because this was the other reason he didn't like his grandma visiting. What she'd just said could have been her being a snob about his local school.

Or it could have been more. It could have been a hint about a possible future.

A possible *after*.

Conor felt the anger rising in the pit of his stomach–

"He's happy where he is, Ma," his mum said, quickly, giving him another look. "Aren't you, Conor?"

Conor gritted his teeth and answered, "I'm fine right where I am."

Dinner was Chinese take-away. Conor's grandma "didn't really cook." This was true. Every time he'd stayed with her, her fridge had held barely anything more than an egg and half an avocado. Conor's mum was still too tired to cook herself, and though

Conor could have made something, it didn't seem to occur to his grandma that this was even a possibility.

He'd been left with the cleanup, though, and he was shoving the foil packages down onto the bag of poisonous berries he'd hidden at the bottom of the rubbish bin when his grandma came in behind him.

"You and I need to have a talk, my boy," she said, standing in the doorway and blocking his escape.

"I have a name, you know," Conor said, pushing down on the bin. "And it's not *my boy*."

"Less of your cheek," his grandma said. She stood there, her arms folded. He stared at her for a minute. She stared back. Then she made a tutting sound. "I'm not your enemy, Conor," she said. "I'm here to help your mother."

"I know why you're here," he said, taking out a cloth to wipe an already clean countertop.

His grandma reached forward and snatched the cloth out of his hand. "I'm here because thirteen-year-old boys shouldn't be wiping down counters without being asked to first."

He glowered back at her. "Were *you* going to do it?"

"Conor—"

"Just go," Conor said. "We don't need you here."

"Conor," she said more firmly, "we need to talk about what's going to happen."

"No, we don't. She's *always* sick after the treatments. She'll be better tomorrow." He glared at her. "And then *you* can go home."

His grandma looked up at the ceiling and sighed. Then she rubbed her face with her hands, and he was surprised to see that she was angry, *really* angry.

But maybe not at him.

He took out another cloth and started wiping again, just so he wouldn't have to look at her. He wiped all the way over to the sink and happened to glance out of the window.

The monster was standing in his backyard, big as the setting sun.

Watching him.

"She'll *seem* better tomorrow," his grandma said, her voice huskier, "but she won't be, Conor."

Well, this was just wrong. He turned back to her. "The treatments are making her better," he said. "That's why she goes."

His grandma just looked at him for a long minute, like she was trying to decide something. "You need to talk to her about this, Conor," she finally said. Then she said, as if to herself, "She needs to talk about this with *you*."

"Talk to me about what?" Conor asked.

His grandma crossed her arms. "About you coming to live with me."

Conor frowned, and for a second the whole room seemed to get darker, for a second it felt like the whole house was shaking, for a second it felt like he could reach down and tear the whole floor right out of the dark and loamy earth –

He blinked. His grandma was still waiting for a response.

"I'm not going to live with you," he said.

"Conor –"

"I'm *never* going to live with you."

"Yes, you are," she said. "I'm sorry, but you are. And I know she's trying to protect you, but I think it's vitally important for you to know that when this is all over, you've got a home, my boy. With someone who'll love you and care for you."

"When this is all over," Conor said, fury in his voice, "you'll leave and we'll be fine."

"Conor –"

And then they both heard from the sitting room, "Mum? *Mum?*"

His grandma rushed out of the kitchen so fast that Conor jumped back in surprise. He could hear his mum coughing and his grandma saying, "It's okay, darling, it's okay, shh, shh, shh." He glanced back out of the kitchen window on his way to the sitting room.

The monster was gone.

His grandma was on the settee, holding on to his mum, rubbing her back as she threw up into a small bucket they kept nearby just in case.

His grandma looked up at him, but her face was set and hard and totally unreadable.

THE WILDNESS OF STORIES

The house was dark. His grandma had finally gotten his mum to bed and then had gone into Conor's bedroom and shut the door, not asking if he wanted anything out of it before she went to sleep herself.

Conor lay awake on the settee. He didn't think he'd be able to sleep, not with the things his grandma had said, not with how his mother had looked tonight. It was three full days after the treatment, about the time she usually started feeling better, except she was still throwing up, still exhausted, for far longer than she should have been –

He pushed the thoughts out of his head but they returned and he had to push them away again. He must have eventually drifted off, but the only way he really knew he was asleep was when the nightmare came.

Not the tree. The *nightmare*.

With the wind roaring and the ground shaking and the hands holding tight but still somehow slipping away, with Conor using all his strength but it still not being enough, with the grip losing itself, with the falling, with the *screaming*–

"NO!" Conor shouted, the terror following him into waking, gripping his chest so hard it felt as if he couldn't breathe, his throat choking, his eyes filling with water.

"No," he said again, more quietly.

The house was silent and dark. He listened for a moment, but nothing stirred, no sound from his mum or his grandma. He squinted through the darkness to the clock on the DVD player.

12:07. Of course it was.

He listened hard into the silence. But nothing happened. He didn't hear his name, he didn't hear the creak of wood.

Maybe it wasn't going to come tonight.

12:08, read the clock.

12:09.

Feeling vaguely angry, Conor got up and went into the kitchen. He looked out of the window.

The monster was standing in his backyard.

What took you so long? it asked.

— · —

It is time for me to tell you the first story, the monster said.

Conor didn't move from the garden chair, where he'd sat himself after he'd gone outside. He had his legs pulled up to his chest and his face pressed into his knees.

Are you listening? the monster asked.

"No," Conor said.

He felt the air swirl around him violently again. *I will be listened to!* started the monster. *I have been alive as long as this land and you will pay the respect owed to me—*

Conor got up from the chair and headed back towards the kitchen door.

Where do you think you're going? demanded the monster.

Conor whirled round, and his face looked so furious, so pained, that the monster actually stood up straight, its huge, leafy eyebrows raising in surprise.

"What do *you* know?" Conor spat. "What do you know about *anything*?"

I know about **you**, *Conor O'Malley,* the monster said.

"No, you don't," Conor said. "If you did, you'd know I don't have time to listen to stupid, boring stories from some stupid, boring tree that isn't even real—"

Oh? said the monster. *Did you dream the berries on the floor of your room?*

"Who cares even if I didn't?!" Conor shouted back. "They're just stupid berries. Woo-hoo, *so scary*. Oh, please, please, save me from the *berries*!"

The monster looked at him quizzically. *How strange*, it said. *The words you say tell me you are scared of the berries, but your actions seem to suggest otherwise.*

"You're as old as the land and you've never heard of sarcasm?" Conor asked.

Oh, I have heard of it, the monster said, putting its huge branch hands on its hips. *But people usually know better than to speak it to me.*

"Can't you just leave me *alone*?"

The monster shook its head, but not in answer to Conor's question. *It is most unusual,* it said. *Nothing I do seems to make you frightened of me.*

"You're just a *tree*," Conor said, and there was no other way he could think about it. Even though it walked and talked, even though it was bigger than his house and could swallow him in one bite, the monster was still, at the end of the day, just a yew tree. Conor could even see more berries growing from the branches at its elbows.

And you have worse things to be frightened of, said the monster, but not as a question.

Conor looked at the ground, then up at the moon, anywhere but at the monster's eyes. The nightmare feeling was rising in him, turning everything around him to darkness, making everything seem heavy and impossible, like he'd been asked to lift a mountain with his bare hands and no one would let him leave until he did.

"I thought," he said, but had to cough before he spoke again. "I saw you watching me earlier when I was fighting with my grandma and I thought . . ."

What did you think? the monster asked when Conor didn't finish.

"Forget it," Conor said, turning back toward the house.

You thought I might be here to help you, the monster said.

Conor stopped.

You thought I might have come to topple your enemies. Slay your dragons.

Conor still didn't look back. But he didn't go inside either.

You felt the truth of it when I said that you had called for me, that you were the reason I had come walking. Did you not?

Conor turned around. "But all you want to do is tell me *stories*," he said, and he couldn't keep the disappointment out of his voice, because it *was* true. He had thought that. He'd *hoped* that.

The monster knelt down so its face was close to Conor's. *Stories of how I toppled enemies,* it said. *Stories of how I slew dragons.*

Conor blinked back at the monster's gaze.

Stories are wild creatures, the monster said. *When you let them loose, who knows what havoc they might wreak?*

The monster looked up, and Conor followed its gaze. It was looking at Conor's bedroom window. The room where his grandma now slept.

Let me tell you a story of when I went walking, the monster said. *Let me tell you of the end of a wicked queen and how I made sure she was never seen again.*

Conor swallowed and looked back at the monster's face.

"Go on," he said.

THE FIRST TALE

Long ago, the monster said, *before this was a town with roads and trains and cars, it was a green place. Trees covered every hill and bordered every path. They shaded every stream and protected every house, for there were houses here even then, made of stone and earth.*

This was a kingdom.

("What?" Conor said, looking around his backyard. *"Here?"*)

(The monster cocked its head at him curiously. *You have not heard of it?*)

("Not a kingdom around here, no," Conor said. "We don't even have a McDonald's.")

Nevertheless, continued the monster, *it was a kingdom, small but happy, for the king was a just king, a man whose wisdom was born out of hardship. His wife had given birth to four strong sons, but in the king's reign, he had been forced to ride into battles to preserve the peace of his kingdom. Battles against giants and dragons, battles against black wolves with red eyes, battles against armies of men led by great wizards.*

These battles secured the kingdom's borders and brought peace to the land. But victory came at a price. One by one, the king's four sons were killed. By the fire of a dragon or the hands of a giant or the teeth of a wolf or the spear of a man. One by one, all four princes of the kingdom fell, leaving the king only one heir. His infant grandson.

("This is all sounding pretty fairy tale-ish," Conor said, suspiciously.)

(*You would not say that if you heard the screams of a man killed by a spear,* said the monster. *Or his cries of terror as he was torn to pieces by wolves. Now be quiet.*)

By and by, the king's wife succumbed to grief, as did the mother of the young prince. The king was left with only the child for company, along with more sadness than one man should bear alone.

"I must remarry," the king decided. "For the good of my prince and of my kingdom, if not for myself."

And remarry he did, to a princess from a neighboring kingdom, a practical union that made both kingdoms stronger. She was young and fair, and though perhaps her face was a bit hard and her tongue a bit sharp, she seemed to make the king happy.

Time passed. The young prince grew until he was nearly a man, coming within two years of the eighteenth birthday that would allow him to ascend to the throne on the old king's death. These were happy days for the kingdom. The battles were over, and the future seemed secure in the hands of the brave young prince.

But one day the king grew ill. Rumor began to spread that he was being poisoned by his new wife. Stories circulated that she had conjured grave magicks to make herself look far younger than she actually was and that beneath her youthful face lurked the scowl of an elderly hag. No one would have put it past her to poison the king, though he begged his subjects until his dying breath not to blame her.

And so he died, with still a year left before his grandson was old enough to take the throne. The queen, his step-grandmother, became regent in his place, and would handle all affairs of state until the prince was old enough to take over.

At first, to the surprise of many, her reign was a good one. Her countenance—despite the rumors—was still youthful and pleasing, and she endeavoured to carry on ruling in the manner of the dead king.

The prince, meanwhile, had fallen in love.

("I *knew* it," Conor grumbled. "These kinds of stories always have stupid princes falling in love." He started walking back to the house. "I thought this was going to be *good*.")

(With one swift movement, the monster grabbed Conor's ankles in a long, strong hand and flipped him upside down, holding him in mid-air so his T-shirt rucked up and his heartbeat thudded in his head.)

(*As I was saying*, said the monster.)

The prince had fallen in love. She was only a farmer's daughter, but she was beautiful, and also smart, as the daughters of farmers need to be, for farms are complicated businesses. The kingdom smiled on the match.

The queen, however, did not. She had enjoyed her time as regent and felt a strange reluctance to give it up. She began to think that *perhaps it was best that the crown remained in the family, that the kingdom be run by those wise enough to do it, and what could be a better solution than for the prince to actually marry **her**?*

("That's disgusting!" Conor said, still upside down. "She was his grandmother!")

(***Step***-*grandmother,* corrected the monster. *Not related by blood, and to all intents and appearances, a young woman herself.*)

(Conor shook his head, his hair dangling. "That's just wrong." He paused a moment. "Can you maybe put me down?")

(The monster lowered him to the ground and continued the story.)

The prince also thought marrying the queen was wrong. He said he would die before doing any such thing. He vowed to run away with the beautiful farmer's daughter and return on his eighteenth birthday to free his people from the tyranny of the queen. And so one night, the prince and the farmer's daughter raced away on horseback, stopping only at dawn to sleep in the shade of a giant yew tree.

("You?" Conor asked.)

(*Me,* the monster said. *But also only part of me. I can take any form of any size, but the yew tree is a shape most comfortable.*)

The prince and the farmer's daughter held each other close in the growing dawn. They had vowed to be chaste until they were able to marry in the next kingdom, but their passions got the better of them, and it was not long before they were asleep and naked in each other's arms.

They slept through the day in the shadows of my branches, and night fell once again. The prince woke. "Arise, my beloved," he whis-pered to the farmer's daughter, "for we ride to the day where we will be man and wife."

But his beloved did not wake. He shook her, and it was only as she slumped back in the moonlight that he noticed the blood staining the ground.

("Blood?" Conor said, but the monster kept talking.)

The prince also had blood covering his own hands, and he saw a bloodied knife on the grass beside them, resting against the roots of the tree. Someone had murdered his beloved and done so in a way that made it look like the prince had committed the crime.

"The queen!" cried the prince. "The queen is responsible for this treachery!"

In the distance, he could hear villagers approaching. If they found him, they would see the knife and the blood, and they would call him murderer. They would put him to death for his crime.

("And the queen would be able to rule unchallenged," Conor said, making a disgusted sound. "I hope this story ends with you ripping her head off.")

There was nowhere for the prince to run. His horse had been chased away while he slept. The yew tree was his only shelter.

And also the only place he could turn for help.

Now, the world was younger then. The barrier between things was thinner, easier to pass through. The prince knew this. And he lifted his head to the great yew tree and he spoke.

(The monster paused.)

("What did he say?" Conor asked.)

(*He said enough to bring me walking,* the monster said. *I know injustice when I see it.*)

The prince ran toward the approaching villagers. "The queen has murdered my bride!" he shouted. "The queen must be stopped!"

The rumors of the queen's witchery had been circulating long enough, and the young prince was so beloved of the people, that it took very little for them to see the obvious truth. It took even less time when they saw the great Green Man walking behind him, high as the hills, coming for vengeance.

(Conor glanced again at the monster's massive arms and legs, at its raggedy, toothy mouth, at its overwhelming *monstrousness.* He imagined what the queen must have thought when she saw it coming.)

(He smiled.)

The subjects stormed the queen's castle with such fury that the stones of its very walls tumbled. Fortifications fell and ceilings collapsed, and when the queen was found in her chambers, the mob seized her and dragged her to the stake right then to burn her alive.

("Good," Conor said, smiling. "She deserved it." He looked up at his bedroom window where his grandmother slept. "I don't suppose you can help me with her?" he asked. "I mean, I don't want to burn her alive or anything, but maybe just—")

The story, said the monster, *is not yet finished.*

THE REST OF THE FIRST TALE

"It's not?" Conor asked. "But the queen was overthrown."

She was, said the monster. *But not by me.*

Conor hesitated, confused. "You said you made sure she was never seen again."

And so I did. When the villagers lit the flames on the stake to burn her alive, I reached in and saved her.

"You *what?*" Conor said.

I took her and carried her far enough away so that the villagers would never find her, far beyond even the kingdom of her birth, to a village by the sea. And there I left her, to live in peace.

Conor got to his feet, his voice rising in disbelief. "But she murdered the farmer's daughter! How could you possibly save a murderer?" Then his face dropped and he took a step back. "You really *are* a monster."

I never said she killed the farmer's daughter, the monster said. *I only said that the **prince** said it was so.*

Conor blinked. Then he crossed his arms. "So who killed her then?"

The monster opened its huge hands in a certain way, and a

breeze blew up, bringing a mist with it.
Conor's house was still behind him, but the
mist covered his backyard, replacing it with a
field with a giant yew in the center and a man
and a woman sleeping at its base.

After their coupling, said the monster,
the prince remained awake.

Conor watched as the young prince rose
and looked down at the sleeping farmer's
daughter, who even Conor could see
was a beauty. The prince watched her for
a moment, then wrapped a blanket around
himself and went to their horse, tied to
one of the yew tree's branches. The prince
retrieved something from the saddlebag, then
untied the horse, slapping it hard on the hind-
quarters to send it running off. The prince held
up what he'd taken out of the bag.

A knife, shining in the moonlight.

"No!" Conor said.

The monster closed its hands and the mist
descended again as the prince approached
the sleeping farmer's daughter,
his knife at the ready.

"You said he was surprised when she didn't wake up!" Conor said.

After he killed the farmer's daughter, said the monster, *the prince lay down next to her and returned to sleep. When he awoke, he acted out a pantomime should anyone be watching. But also, it may surprise you to learn, for himself.* The monster's branches creaked. *Sometimes people need to lie to themselves most of all.*

"You said he asked for your help! And that you *gave* it!"

I only said he told me enough to make me come walking.

Conor looked wide-eyed from the monster to his backyard, which was reemerging from the dissipating mist. "What did he tell you?" he asked.

He told me that he had done it for the good of the kingdom. That the new queen was in fact a witch, that his grandfather had suspected it to be true when he married her, but that he had overlooked it because of her beauty. The prince couldn't topple a powerful witch on his own. He needed the fury of the villagers to help him. The death of the farmer's daughter saw to that. He was sorry to do it. Heartbroken, he said, but as his own father had died in defence of the kingdom, so did his fair maiden. Her death was serving to overthrow a great evil. When he said that the queen had murdered his bride, he believed, in his own way, that it was actually true.

"That's a load of crap!" Conor shouted. "He didn't need to kill her. The people were behind him. They would have followed him anyway."

The justifications of men who kill should always be heard with skepticism, said the monster. *And so the injustice that I saw, the reason that I came walking, was for the queen, not the prince.*

"Did he ever get caught?" Conor said, aghast. "Did they punish him?"

He became a much beloved king, the monster said, *who ruled happily until the end of his long days.*

Conor looked up to his bedroom window, frowning again. "So the good prince was a murderer and the evil queen wasn't a witch after all. Is that supposed to be the lesson of all this? That I should be *nice* to her?"

He heard a strange rumbling, different from before, and it took him a minute to realize the monster was *laughing.*

*You think I tell you stories to teach you **lessons?*** the monster said. *You think I have come walking out of time and earth itself to teach you a **lesson** in niceness?*

It laughed louder and louder again, until the ground was shaking and it felt like the sky itself might tumble down.

"Yeah, all right," Conor said, embarrassed.

No, no, the monster said, finally calming itself. *The queen most certainly **was** a witch and could very well have been on her way to great evil. Who's to say? She was trying to hold on to power, after all.*

"Why did you save her then?"

*Because what she was **not,** was a murderer.*

Conor walked around the garden a bit, thinking. Then he did it a bit more. "I don't understand. Who's the good guy here?"

There is not always a good guy. Nor is there always a bad one. Most people are somewhere in between.

Conor shook his head. "That's a terrible story. And a cheat."

*It is a **true** story,* the monster said. *Many things that are true feel like a cheat. Kingdoms get the princes they deserve, farmers' daughters die for no reason, and sometimes witches merit saving. Quite often, actually. You'd be surprised.*

Conor glanced up at his bedroom window again, imagining his grandma sleeping in his bed. "So how is that supposed to save me from her?"

The monster stood to its full height, looking down on Conor from afar.

*It is not **her** you need saving from,* it said.

Conor sat up straight on the settee, breathing heavily again.

12:07, read the clock.

"Dammit!" Conor said. "Am I dreaming or not?"

He stood up angrily—

And immediately stubbed his toe.

"What *now*?" he grumbled, leaning over to flick on a light.

From a knot in a floorboard, a fresh, new and very solid sapling had sprouted, about a foot tall.

Conor stared at it for a while. Then he went to the kitchen to get a knife to saw it out of the floor.

UNDERSTANDING

"I forgive you," Lily said, catching up with him on the walk to school the following day.

"For what?" Conor asked, not looking at her. He was still irritated at the monster's story, from the cheating and twisting way it went, none of which was any help at all. He'd spent half an hour sawing the surprisingly tough sapling out of the floor and had felt as though he'd barely fallen asleep again before it was time to get up, something he'd only found out because his grandma had started yelling at him for being late. She wouldn't even let him say good-bye to his mum, who she said had had a rough night and needed her rest. Which made him feel guilty because if his mum had had a rough night, then *he* should have been there to help her, not his grandma who had barely let him brush his teeth before shoving an apple in his hand and pushing him out of the door.

"I forgive you for getting me in trouble, stupid," Lily said, but not too harshly.

"You got yourself in trouble," Conor said. "You're the one who pushed Sully over."

"I forgive you for *lying*," Lily said, her poodly curls shoved painfully back into a band.

Conor just kept on walking.

"Aren't you going to say you're sorry back?" Lily asked.

"Nope," Conor said.

"Why not?"

"Because I'm *not* sorry."

"Conor–"

"I'm not sorry," Conor said, stopping, "and *I* don't forgive *you*."

They glared at each other in the cool morning sun, neither wanting to be the first to look away.

"My mum said we need to make allowances for you," Lily finally said. "Because of what you're going through."

And for a moment, the sun seemed to go behind the clouds. For a moment, all Conor could see was sudden thunderstorms on the way, could *feel* them ready to explode in the sky and through his body and out of his fists. For a moment, he felt as if he could grab hold of the very air and twist it around Lily and rip her right in two–

"Conor?" Lily said, looking startled.

"Your mum doesn't know *anything*," he said. "And neither do you."

He walked away from her, fast, leaving her behind.

—— • ——

It was just over a year ago that Lily had told a few of her friends about Conor's mum, even though he hadn't said she could. Those friends told a few more, who told a few more, and before the day was half through, it was like a circle had opened around him, a dead area with Conor at the center, surrounded by land mines that everyone was afraid to walk through. All of a sudden, the people he'd thought were his friends would stop talking when he came over, not that there were so very many beyond Lily anyway, but *still*. He'd catch people whispering as he walked by in the corridor or at lunch. Even teachers would get a different look on their faces when he put up his hand during lessons.

So eventually he stopped going over to groups of friends, stopped looking up at the whispers, and even stopped putting up his hand.

Not that anyone seemed to notice. It was like he'd suddenly turned invisible.

He'd never had a harder year of school or been more relieved for a summer holiday to come around than this last one. His mother was deep into her treatments, which she'd said over and over again were rough but "doing the job," the long schedule of them nearing its end. The plan was that she'd finish them, a new school year would start, and they'd be able to put all this behind them and start afresh.

Except it hadn't worked out that way. His mum's treatments had carried on longer than they'd originally thought, first a second round and now a third. The teachers in his new year were even worse because they only knew him in terms of his mum and not who he was before. And the other kids still treated him like *he* was the one who was ill, especially since Harry and his cronies had singled him out.

And now his grandma was hanging around the house and he was dreaming about trees.

Or maybe it *wasn't* a dream. Which would actually be worse.

He walked on angrily to school. He blamed Lily because it *was* mostly her fault, wasn't it?

He blamed Lily, because who else was there?

This time, Harry's fist was in his stomach.

Conor fell to the ground, scraping his knee on the concrete step, tearing a hole in his uniform trousers. The hole was the worst part of it. He was terrible at sewing.

"Are you sick or something, O'Malley?" Sully said, laughing behind him somewhere. "It's like you fall every day."

"You should go to a doctor for that," he heard Anton say.

"Maybe he's drunk," Sully said, and there was more laughter, except for a silent spot between them where Conor knew Harry wasn't laughing. He knew, without looking back, that Harry was just watching him, waiting to see what he would do.

As he stood, he saw Lily against the school wall. She was

with some other girls, heading back inside at the end of break time. She wasn't talking to them, just looking at Conor as she walked away.

"No help from Super Poodle today," Sully said, still laughing.

"Lucky for you, Sully," Harry said, speaking for the first time. Conor still hadn't turned back to face them, but he could tell Harry wasn't laughing at Sully's joke. Conor watched Lily until she was gone.

"Hey, *look* at us when we're talking to you," Sully said, burning from Harry's comment no doubt and grabbing Conor's shoulder, spinning him around.

"Don't touch him," Harry said, calm and low, but so ominously that Sully immediately stepped back. "O'Malley and I have an understanding," Harry said. "I'm the only one who touches him. Isn't that right?"

Conor waited for a moment and then slowly nodded. That did seem to be the understanding.

Harry, his face still blank, his eyes still locked on Conor's, stepped up close to him. Conor didn't flinch, and they stood, eye-to-eye, while Anton and Sully looked at each other a bit nervously.

Harry cocked his head slightly, as if a question had occurred to him, one he was trying to puzzle out. Conor still didn't move. The rest of their class had already gone inside. He could feel the quiet opening up around them, even Anton and Sully falling silent. They would have to go soon. They needed to go *now*.

But nobody moved.

Harry raised a fist and pulled it back as if to swing it at Conor's face.

Conor still didn't flinch. He didn't even move. He just stared into Harry's eyes, waiting for the punch to fall.

But it didn't.

Harry lowered his fist, dropping it slowly down by his side, still staring at Conor. "Yes," he finally said, quietly, as if he'd worked something out. "That's what I thought."

And then, once more, came the voice of doom.

"You boys!" Miss Kwan called, coming across the yard toward them like terror on two legs. "Break was over three minutes ago! What do you think you're still doing out here?"

"Sorry, Miss," Harry said, his voice suddenly light. "We were discussing Mrs. Marl's Life Writing homework with Conor and lost track of time." He slapped a hand on Conor's shoulder as if they were lifelong friends. "No one knows about stories like Conor here." He nodded seriously at Miss Kwan. "And talking about it helps get him out of himself."

"Yes," Miss Kwan frowned, "that sounds entirely likely. Everyone here is on first warning. One more problem today, and that's detention for all of you."

"Yes, Miss," Harry said brightly, with Anton and Sully

mumbling the same. They trudged off back to lessons, Conor following in step just behind.

"A moment please, Conor," Miss Kwan said.

He stopped and turned to her but didn't look up at her face.

"Are you sure everything's all right between you and those boys?" Miss Kwan said, putting her voice into its "kindly" mode, which was only slightly less scary than full-on shouting.

"Yes, Miss," Conor said, still not looking at her.

"Because I'm not blind to how Harry works, you know," she said. "A bully with charisma and top marks is still a bully." She sighed, annoyed. "He'll probably end up Prime Minister one day. God help us all."

Conor said nothing, and the silence took on a particular quality, one he was familiar with, caused by how Miss Kwan's body shifted forward, her shoulders dropping, her head leaning down toward Conor's.

He knew what was coming. He knew and hated it.

"I can't imagine what you must be going through, Conor,"

Miss Kwan said, so quiet it was almost a whisper, "but if you ever want to talk, my door is always open."

He couldn't look at her, couldn't see the care there, couldn't *bear* to hear it in her voice.

(Because he didn't deserve it.)

(The nightmare flashed in him, the screaming and the terror, and what happened at the end−)

"I'm fine, Miss," he mumbled, looking at his shoes. "I'm not going through anything."

After a second, he heard Miss Kwan sigh again. "All right then," she said. "Forget about the first warning and come back inside." She patted him once on the shoulder and recrossed the yard to the doors.

And for a moment, Conor was entirely alone.

He knew right then he could probably stay out there all day and no one would punish him for it.

Which somehow made him feel even worse.

LITTLE TALK

After school, his grandma was waiting for him on the settee.

"We need to have a talk," she said before he even got the door shut, and there was a look on her face that made him stop. A look that made his stomach hurt.

"What's wrong?" he asked.

His grandmother took in a long, loud breath through her nose and stared out of the front window, as if gathering herself. She looked like a bird of prey. A hawk that could carry off a sheep.

"Your mother has to go back to the hospital," she said. "You're going to come and stay with me for a few days. You'll need to pack a bag."

Conor didn't move. "What's wrong with her?"

His grandma's eyes widened for just a second, as if she couldn't believe he was asking a question so cataclysmically stupid. Then she relented. "There's a lot of pain," she said. "More than there should be."

"She's got medicine for her pain—" Conor started, but his grandmother clapped her hands together, just the once, but *loud*, loud enough to stop him.

74

"It's not working, Conor," she said, crisply, and it seemed like she was looking just over his head rather than at him. "It's not working."

"What's not working?"

His grandma tapped her hands together lightly a few more times, like she was testing them out or something, then she looked out of the window again, all the while keeping her mouth firmly shut. She finally stood, concentrating on smoothing down her dress.

"Your mum's upstairs," she said. "She wants to talk to you."

"But–"

"Your father's flying in on Sunday."

He straightened up. "*Dad's* coming?"

"I've got some calls to make," she said, stepping past him and out of the front door, taking out her mobile.

"Why is Dad coming?" he called after her.

"Your mum's waiting," she said, pulling the front door shut behind her.

Conor hadn't even had a chance to put down his rucksack.

His father was coming. His *father*. From *America*. Who hadn't come since the Christmas before last. Whose new wife always seemed to suffer emergencies at the last minute that kept him from visiting more often, especially now that the baby was born. His father, who Conor had grown used to not having around as the trips grew less frequent and the phone calls got further and further apart.

His father was coming.

Why?

"Conor?" he heard his mum call.

She wasn't in her room. She was in *his,* lying back on his bed on top of the duvet, gazing out of the window to the churchyard up the hill.

And the yew tree.

Which was just a yew tree.

"Hey, darling," she said, smiling at him from where she lay, but he could tell by the lines around her eyes that she really was hurting, hurting like he'd only seen her hurt once before. She'd had to go to the hospital then as well and hadn't come out for nearly two weeks. It had been last Easter, and the weeks at his grandma's had almost been the death of them both.

"What's the matter?" he asked. "Why are you going back to the hospital?"

She patted the duvet next to her to get him to come and sit down.

He stayed where he was. "What's wrong?"

She still smiled but it was tighter now, and she traced her fingers along the threaded pattern of the duvet, grizzly bears that Conor had outgrown years ago. She had tied her red rose scarf around her head, but only loosely, and he could see her pale scalp underneath. He didn't think she'd even pretended to try on any of his grandma's old wigs.

"I'm going to be okay," she said. "I really am."

"Are you?" he asked.

"We've been here before, Conor," she said. "So don't worry. I've felt really bad and I've gone in and they've taken care of it. That's what'll happen this time." She patted the duvet cover again. "Won't you come and sit down next to your tired old mum?"

Conor swallowed, but her smile was brighter and—he could tell—it was a real one. He went over and sat next to her on the side facing the window. She ran her hand through his hair, lifting it out of his eyes, and he could see how skinny her arm was, almost like it was just bone and skin.

"Why is Dad coming?" he asked.

His mother paused, then put her hand back down into her lap. "It's been a while since you've seen him. Aren't you excited?"

"Grandma doesn't seem too happy."

His mother snorted. "Well, you know how she feels about your dad. Don't listen to her. Enjoy his visit."

They sat in silence for a moment. "There's something else," Conor finally said. "Isn't there?"

He felt his mother sit up a little straighter on her pillow. "Look at me, son," she said, gently.

He turned his head to look at her, though he would have paid any amount of money not to have to do it.

"This latest treatment's not doing what it's supposed to," she said. "All that means is they're going to have to adjust it, try something else."

"Is that it?" Conor asked.

She nodded. "That's it. There's lots more they can do. It's normal. Don't worry."

"You're sure?"

"I'm sure."

"Because," and here Conor stopped for a second and looked down at the floor. "Because you could tell me, you know."

And then he felt her arms around him, her thin, thin arms that used to be so soft when she hugged him. She didn't say anything, just held on to him. He went back to looking out of the window and after a moment, his mother turned to look, too.

"That's a yew tree, you know," she finally said.

Conor rolled his eyes, but not in a bad way. "Yes, Mum, you've told me a hundred times."

"Keep an eye on it for me while I'm away, will you?" she said. "Make sure it's still here when I get back?"

And Conor knew this was her way of telling him she *was* coming back, so all he did was nod, and they both kept looking out at the tree.

Which stayed a tree, no matter how long they looked.

GRANDMA'S HOUSE

Five days. The monster hadn't come for five days.

Maybe it didn't know where his grandma lived. Or maybe it was just too far to come. She didn't have much of a yard anyway, even though her house was *way* bigger than Conor and his mum's. She'd crammed her backyard with sheds and a stone pond and a wood-paneled "office" she'd had installed across the back half, where she did most of her real-estate agent work, a job so boring Conor never listened past the first sentence of her description of it. Everything else was just brick paths and flowers in pots. No room for a tree at all. It didn't even have *grass*.

"Don't stand there gawping, young man," his grandma said, leaning out of the back door and hooking in an earring. "Your dad'll be here soon, and I'm going to see your mum."

"I wasn't gawping," Conor said.

"What's that got to do with the price of milk? Come inside."

She vanished into the house, and he slowly trudged after her. It was Sunday, the day his father would be arriving from the airport. He would come here and pick up Conor, they'd go and see his mum, and then they'd spend some "father-son" time

80

together. Conor was almost certain this was code for another round of We Need To Have A Talk.

His grandma wouldn't be here when his father arrived. Which suited everyone.

"Pick up your rucksack from the front hall, please," she said, stepping past him and grabbing her handbag. "No need for him to think I'm keeping you in a pigsty."

"Not much chance of that," Conor muttered as she went to the hall mirror to check her lipstick.

His grandma's house was cleaner than his mum's hospital room. Her cleaning lady, Marta, came on Wednesdays, but Conor didn't see why she bothered. His grandma would get up first thing in the morning to vacuum, did laundry four times a week, and once cleaned the bath at midnight before going to bed. She wouldn't let dinner dishes touch the sink on their way to the dishwasher, once even taking a plate Conor was still eating from.

"A woman my age, living alone," she said, at least once a day, "if I don't keep on top of things, who will?"

She said it like a challenge, as if defying Conor to answer.

She drove him to school, and he got there early every single day, even though it was a forty-five minute drive. She was also waiting for him every day after school when he left, taking them both straight to the hospital to see his mum. They'd stay for an hour or so, less if his mum was too tired to talk—which had happened twice out of the previous five days—and then go home to his grandma's house, where she'd make him do his homework while she ordered whatever take-out they hadn't already eaten so far.

It was like the time Conor and his mum had stayed in a bed-and-breakfast one summer in Cornwall. Except cleaner. And bossier.

"Now, Conor," she said, slipping on her suit jacket. It was a Sunday but she didn't have any houses to show, so he wasn't sure why she was dressing up so much just to go to the hospital. He suspected it probably had something to do with making his dad uncomfortable.

"Your father may not notice how tired your mum's been getting, okay?" she said. "So we're going to have to work together to make sure he doesn't overstay his welcome." She checked herself in the mirror again and lowered her voice. "Not that *that*'s been a problem."

She turned, gave him a flash of starfish hand as a wave, and said, "Be good."

The door clattered shut behind her. Conor was alone in her house.

He went up to the guest room where he slept. His grandma kept calling it *his* room, but he only ever called it the guest room, which always made his grandmother shake her head and mumble to herself.

But what did she expect? It didn't *look* like his room. It didn't look like *anybody's* room, certainly not a boy's. The walls were bare white except for three different prints of sailing ships, which was probably as far as his grandma's thinking went toward what boys might like. The sheets and duvet covers were a bright, blinding white, too, and the only other piece of furniture was an oak cabinet big enough to have lunch in.

It could have been any room in any home on any planet anywhere. He didn't even like *being* in it, not even to get away from his grandma. He'd only come up now to get a book since his grandma had forbidden handheld computer games from her house. He fished one out of his bag and made to leave, glancing out of the window to the backyard as he went.

Still just stone paths and sheds and the office.

Nothing looking back at him at all.

The sitting room was one of those sitting rooms where no one ever actually sat. Conor wasn't allowed in there at any time, lest he smudge the upholstery somehow, so of course this was where he went to read his book while he waited for his father.

He slumped down on her settee, which had curved wooden legs so thin it looked like it was wearing high heels. There was a glass-fronted cabinet opposite, filled with plates on display stands

and teacups with so many curlicues it was a wonder you could drink from them without cutting your lips. Hanging over the mantelpiece was his grandma's prize clock, which no one but her could ever touch. Handed down from her own mother, Conor's grandma had threatened for years to take it on *Antiques Roadshow* to get it valued. It had a proper pendulum swinging underneath it, and it chimed, too, every fifteen minutes, loud enough to make you jump if you weren't expecting it.

The whole room was like a museum of how people lived in olden times. There wasn't even a television. That was in the kitchen and almost never switched on.

He read. What else was there to do?

He had hoped to talk to his father before he flew out, but what with the hospital visits and the time difference and the new wife's convenient migraines, he was just going to have to see him when he showed up.

Whenever that would be. Conor looked at the pendulum clock. Twelve forty-two, it said. It would chime in three minutes.

Three empty, quiet minutes.

He realized he was actually nervous. It had been a long time since he'd seen his father in person and not just on Skype. Would he look different? Would *Conor* look different?

And then there were the other questions. Why was he coming *now*? His mum didn't look great, looked even worse after five days in hospital, but she was still hopeful about the new medicine she was being given. Christmas was still months away and Conor's birthday was already past. So why now?

He looked at the floor, the center of which was covered in a very expensive, very old-looking oval rug. He reached down and lifted up an edge of it, looking at the polished boards beneath. There was a knot in one of them. He ran his fingers over it, but the board was so old and smooth, you couldn't tell the difference between the knot and the rest of it.

"Are you in there?" Conor whispered.

He jumped as the doorbell rang. He scrambled up and out of the sitting room, feeling more excited than he'd thought he would. He opened the front door.

There was his father, looking totally different but exactly the same.

"Hey, son," his dad said, his voice bending in that weird way that America had started to shape it.

Conor smiled wider than he had for at least a year.

CHAMP

"How you hanging in there, champ?" his father asked him while they waited for the waitress to bring them their pizzas.

"Champ?" Conor asked, raising a skeptical eyebrow.

"Sorry," his father said, smiling bashfully. "America is almost a whole different language."

"Your voice sounds funnier every time I talk to you."

"Yeah, well." His father fidgeted with his wineglass. "It's good to see you."

Conor took a drink of his Coke. His mum had been really poorly when they'd gotten to the hospital. They'd had to wait for his grandma to help her out of the bathroom, and then she was so tired all she was really able to say was "Hi, sweetheart," to Conor and "Hello, Liam," to his father before falling back to sleep. His grandma ushered them out moments later, a look on her face that even his dad wasn't going to argue with.

"Your mother is, uh," his father said now, squinting at nothing in particular. "She's a fighter, isn't she?"

Conor shrugged.

"So, how are *you* holding up, Con?"

86

"That's like the eight hundredth time you've asked me since you got here," Conor said.

"Sorry," his father said.

"I'm *fine*," Conor said. "Mum's on this new medicine. It'll make her better. She looks bad, but she's looked bad before. Why is everyone acting like –?"

He stopped and took another drink of his Coke.

"You're right, son," his father said. "You're absolutely right." He turned his wineglass slowly around once on the table. "Still," he said. "You're going to need to be brave for her, Con. You're going to need to be real, real brave for her."

"You talk like American television."

His father laughed, quietly. "Your sister's doing well. Almost walking."

"*Half*-sister," Conor said.

"I can't wait for you to meet her," his father said. "We'll have to arrange for a visit soon. Maybe even this Christmas. Would you like that?"

Conor met his father's eyes. "What about Mum?"

"I've talked it over with your grandma. She seemed to think it wasn't a bad idea, as long as we got you back in time for the new school term."

Conor ran a hand along the edge of the table. "So it'd just be a visit then?"

"What do you mean?" his father said, sounding surprised.

"A visit as opposed to . . ." He trailed off, and Conor knew he'd worked out what he meant. "Conor—"

But Conor suddenly didn't want him to finish. "There's a tree that's been visiting me," he said, talking quickly, starting to peel the label off the Coke bottle. "It comes to the house at night, tells me stories."

His father blinked, baffled. *What?*

"I thought it was a dream at first," Conor said, scratching at the label with his thumbnail, "but then I kept finding leaves when I woke up and little trees growing out of the floor. I've been hiding them all so no one will find out."

"Conor—"

"It hasn't come to grandma's house yet. I was thinking she might live too far away—"

"What are you—?"

"But why should it matter if it's all a dream, though? Why wouldn't a dream be able to walk across town? Not if it's as old as the earth and as big as the world—"

"Conor, *stop* this—"

"I don't want to live with grandma," Conor said, his voice suddenly strong and filled with a thickness that felt like it was choking him. He kept his eyes firmly on the Coke bottle label, his thumbnail scraping the wet paper away. "Why can't I come and live with you? Why can't I come to America?"

His father licked his lips. "You mean when—"

"Grandma's house is an old lady's house," Conor said.

His father gave another small laugh. "I'll be sure to tell her you called her an old lady."

"You can't touch anything or sit anywhere," Conor said. "You can't leave a mess for even two seconds. And she's only got Internet out in her office and I'm not allowed in there."

"I'm sure we can talk to her about those things. I'm sure there's lots of room to make it easier, make you comfortable there."

"I don't *want* to be comfortable there!" Conor said, raising his voice. "I want my own room in my own house."

"You wouldn't have that in America," his father said. "We barely have room for the three of us, Con. Your grandma has a lot more money and space than we do. Plus, you're in school here, your friends are here, your whole *life* is here. It would be unfair to just take you out of all that."

"Unfair to who?" Conor asked.

His father sighed. "This is what I meant," he said. "This is what I meant when I said you were going to have to be brave."

"That's what everyone says," Conor said. "As if it means anything."

"I'm sorry," his father said. "I know it seems really unfair, and I wish it was different—"

"Do you?"

"Of *course* I do." His father leaned in over the table. "But this way is best. You'll see."

Conor swallowed, still not meeting his eye. Then he swallowed again. "Can we can talk about it more when Mum gets better?"

His father slowly sat back in his chair again. "Of course we can, buddy. That's exactly what we'll do."

Conor looked at him again. *"Buddy?"*

His father smiled. "Sorry." He lifted his wineglass and took a drink long enough to drain the whole glass. He set it down with a small gasp, then he gave Conor a quizzical look. "What was all that you were saying about a tree?"

But the waitress came and silence fell as she put their pizzas in front of them. "Americano," Conor frowned, looking down at his. "If it could talk, I wonder if it would sound like you."

AMERICANS DON'T GET
MUCH HOLIDAY

"Doesn't look like your grandma's home yet," Conor's father said, pulling up the rental car in front of her house.

"She sometimes goes back to the hospital after I go to bed," Conor said. "The nurses let her sleep in a chair."

His dad nodded. "She may not like me," he said, "but that doesn't mean she's a bad lady."

Conor stared out of the window at her house. "How long are you here for?" he asked. He'd been afraid to ask before now.

His father let out a long breath, the kind of breath that said bad news was coming. "Just a few days, I'm afraid."

Conor turned to him. "That's *all*?"

"Americans don't get much holiday."

"You're not American."

"But I live there now." He grinned. "You're the one who made fun of my accent all night."

"Why did you come then?" Conor asked. "Why bother coming at all?"

His father waited a moment before answering. "I came

because your mum asked me to." He looked like he was going to say more, but he didn't.

Conor didn't say anything either.

"I'll come back, though," his father said. "You know, when I need to." His voice brightened. "And you'll visit us at Christmas! That'll be good fun."

"In your cramped house where there's no room for me," Conor said.

"Conor—"

"And then I'll come back here for school."

"Con—"

"Why did you come?" Conor asked again, his voice low.

His father didn't answer. A silence opened up in the car that felt like they were sitting on opposite sides of a canyon. Then his father reached out a hand for Conor's shoulder, but Conor ducked it and pulled on the door handle to get out.

"Conor, *wait.*"

Conor waited but didn't turn around.

"You want me to come in until she gets home?" his father asked. "Keep you company?"

"I'm fine on my own," Conor said, and got out of the car.

The house was quiet when he got inside. Why wouldn't it be?

He was alone.

He slumped on the expensive settee again, listening to it creak as he fell back into it. It was such a satisfying sound that he got up and slumped back down into it again. Then he got back up and jumped on it, the wooden legs moaning as they scraped a few inches across the floor, leaving four identical scratches on the hardwood.

He smiled to himself. That felt *good*.

He jumped off and gave the settee a kick to push it back even further. He was barely aware that he was breathing heavily. His head felt hot, almost like he had a fever. He raised a foot to kick the settee again.

Then he looked up and saw the clock.

His grandma's precious clock, hanging over the mantelpiece, the pendulum swinging back and forth, back and forth, like it was getting on with its own, private life, not caring about Conor at all.

He approached it slowly, his fists clenched. It was only a moment before it would *bong bong bong* its way to nine o'clock. Conor stood there until the second hand glided around and reached the twelve. The instant the *bong*s were about to start, he grabbed the pendulum, holding it at the high point of its swing.

He could hear the mechanism of the clock complaining as the first *b* of the interrupted *bong* hovered in the air. With his free hand, Conor reached up and pushed the minute and second hands forward from the twelve. They resisted but he pushed harder, hearing a loud *click* as he did so that didn't sound especially good. The minute and second hands sprung suddenly free from whatever was holding them back, and Conor spun them around, catching up with the hour hand and taking it along, too, hearing more complaining half-*bong*s and painful *click*s from deep inside the wooden case.

He could feel drops of sweat gathering on his forehead, and his chest felt like it was glowing with heat.

(–almost like being in the nightmare, that same feverish blur of the world slipping off its axis, but this time *he* was the one in control, this time *he* was the nightmare–)

The second hand, the thinnest of the three, suddenly snapped and fell out of the clockface completely, bouncing once on the rug and disappearing into the ashes of the hearth.

Conor stepped back quickly, letting go of the pendulum. It dropped to its center point but didn't start swinging again. Nor did the clock make any of the whirring, ticking sounds it usually made as it ran, its hands now frozen solidly in place.

Uh-oh.

Conor's stomach started squeezing as he realized what he'd done.

Oh, no, he thought.

Oh, *no*.

He'd broken it.

A clock that was probably worth more than his mum's whole beaten-up car.

His grandma was going to kill him, maybe actually, literally *kill* him –

Then he noticed.

The hour and minute hands had stopped at a specific time.

12:07.

As destruction goes, the monster said behind him, *this is all remarkably pitiful.*

Conor whirled around. Somehow, some way, the monster was in his grandma's sitting room. It was far too big, of course, having to bend down very, very low to fit under the ceiling, its branches and leaves twisting together tighter and tighter to make it smaller, but here it was, filling up every corner.

*It is the kind of destruction I would expect from a **boy**,* it said, its breath blowing back Conor's hair.

"What are you doing here?" Conor asked. He felt a sudden surge of hope. "Am I asleep? Is this a dream? Like when you broke my bedroom window and I woke up and–"

I have come to tell you the second tale, the monster said.

Conor made an exasperated sound and looked back at the broken clock. "Is it going to be as bad as the last one?" he asked, distractedly.

It ends in proper destruction, if that is what you mean.

Conor turned back to the monster. Its face had rearranged itself into the expression Conor recognized as the evil grin.

"Is it a cheating story?" Conor asked. "Does it sound like it's going to be one way and then it's a total other way?"

No, said the monster. *It is about a man who thought only of himself.* The monster smiled again, looking even more wicked. *And he gets punished very, very badly indeed.*

Conor stood breathing for a second, thinking about the broken clock, about the scratches on the hardwood, about the poisonous berries dropping from the monster onto his grandma's clean floor.

He thought about his father.

"I'm listening," Conor said.

THE SECOND TALE

One hundred and fifty years ago, the monster began, *this country had become a place of industry. Factories grew on the landscape like weeds. Trees fell, fields were up-ended, rivers blackened. The sky choked on smoke and ash, and the people did, too, spending their days coughing and itching, their eyes turned forever toward the ground. Villages grew into towns, towns into cities. And people began to live* **on** *the earth rather than* **within** *it.*

But there was still green, if you knew where to look.

(The monster opened its hands again, and a mist rolled through his grandma's sitting room. When it cleared, Conor and the monster stood on a field of green, overlooking a valley of metal and brick.)

("So I *am* asleep," Conor said.)

(*Quiet*, said the monster. *Here he comes.* And Conor saw a sour-looking man with heavy black clothes and a deep, deep frown climbing the hill toward them.)

Along the edge of this green lived a man. His name is not important, as no one ever used it. The villagers only ever called him the Apothecary.

("The what?" Conor asked.)

(*The Apothecary,* said the monster.)

("The what?")

Apothecary was an old-fashioned name, even then, for a chemist.

("Oh," Conor said. "Why didn't you just say?")

But the name was well-earned, because apothecaries were ancient, dealing in the old ways of medicine, too. Of herbs and barks, of concoctions brewed from berries and leaves.

("Dad's new wife does that," Conor said as they watched the man dig up a root. "She owns a shop that sells crystals.")

(The monster frowned. *It is not remotely the same.*)

Many a day the Apothecary went walking to collect the herbs and leaves of the surrounding green. But as the years passed, his walks became longer and longer as the factories and roads sprawled out of town like one of the rashes he was so effective in treating. Where he used to be able to collect paxsfoil and bella rosa before morning tea, it began to take him the entire day.

*The world was changing, and the Apothecary grew bitter. Or rather, **more** bitter, for he had always been an unpleasant man. He was greedy and charged too much for his cures, often taking more than the patient could afford to pay. Nevertheless, he was surprised at how unloved he was by the villagers, thinking they should treat him with far more respect. And because his attitude was poor, their attitude toward him was also poor, until, as time went on, his patients began seeking other, more modern remedies from other, more modern healers. Which only, of course, made the Apothecary even more bitter.*

(The mist surrounded them again, and the scene changed. They were now standing on a lawn atop a small hillock. A parsonage sat to one side and a great yew tree stood in the middle of a few new headstones.)

In the Apothecary's village there also lived a parson —

("This is the hill behind my house," Conor interrupted. He looked around, but there was no railway line yet, no rows of houses, just a few footpaths and a mucky riverbed.)

The parson had two daughters, the monster went on, *who were the light of his life.*

(Two young girls came screaming out of the parsonage, giggling and laughing and trying to hit each other with handfuls of grass. They ran around the trunk of the yew tree, hiding from each other.)

("That's you," Conor said, pointing at the tree, which for the moment was just a tree.)

Yes, fine, on the parsonage grounds, there also grew a yew tree.

(*And a very handsome yew tree it was,* said the monster.)

("If you say so yourself," Conor said.)

Now, the Apothecary wanted the yew tree very badly.

("He did?" Conor asked. "Why?")

(The monster looked surprised. *The yew tree is the most important of all the healing trees,* it said. *It lives for thousands of years. Its berries, its bark, its leaves, its sap, its pulp, its wood, they all thrum and burn and twist with life. It can cure almost any ailment man suffers from, mixed and treated by the right apothecary.*)

(Conor furrowed his forehead. "You're making that up.")

(The monster's face went stormy. *You dare to question* me, *boy?*)

("No," Conor said, stepping back at the monster's anger. "I've just never heard that before.")

(The monster frowned angrily for a moment longer, then got on with the story.)

In order to harvest these things from the tree, the Apothecary would have had to cut it down. And this the parson would not allow. The yew had stood on this ground long before it was set aside for the church. A graveyard was already starting to be used and a new church building was in the planning stages. The yew would protect the church from the heavy rains and the harshest weather, and the parson—no matter how often the Apothecary asked, for he did ask very often—would not allow the Apothecary anywhere near the tree.

Now, the parson was an enlightened man, and a kind one. He wanted the very best for his congregation, to take them out of the dark ages of superstition and witchery. He preached against the Apothecary's use of the old ways, and the Apothecary's foul temper and greed made certain these sermons fell on eager ears. His business shrank even further.

But then one day, the parson's daughters fell sick. First the one, and then the other, with an infection that swept the countryside.

(The sky darkened, and Conor could hear the coughing of the daughters within the parsonage, could also hear the loud praying of the parson and the tears of the parson's wife.)

Nothing the parson did helped. No prayer, no cure from the modern doctor two towns over, no remedies of the field offered shyly and secretly by his parishioners. Nothing. The daughters wasted away and approached death. Finally, there was no other option but to approach the Apothecary. The parson swallowed his pride and went to beg the Apothecary's forgiveness.

"Won't you help my daughters?" the parson asked, down on his

knees at the Apothecary's front door. "If not for me, then for my two innocent girls."

"Why should I?" the Apothecary asked. "You have driven away my business with your preachings. You have refused me the yew tree, my best source of healing. You have turned this village against me."

"You may have the yew tree," the parson said. "I will preach sermons in your favor. I will send my parishioners to you for their every ailment. You may have anything you like, if you would only save my daughters."

The Apothecary was surprised. "You would give up everything you believed in?"

"If it would save my daughters," the parson said. "I'd give up everything."

"Then," the Apothecary said, shutting his door on the parson, "there is nothing I can do to help you."

("What?" Conor said.)

That very night, both of the parson's daughters died.

(*"What?"* Conor said again, the nightmare feeling taking hold of his guts.)

And that very night, I came walking.

("Good!" Conor shouted. "That stupid git deserves all the punishment he gets.")

(*I thought so, too,* said the monster.)

It was shortly after midnight that I tore the parson's home from its very foundations.

THE REST OF THE SECOND TALE

Conor whirled round. "The *parson?*"

Yes, said the monster. *I flung his roof into the dell below and knocked down every wall of his house with my fists.*

The parson's house was still before them, and Conor saw the yew tree next to it awaken into the monster and set ferociously on the parsonage. With the first blow to the roof, the front door flew open, and the parson and his wife fled in terror. The monster in the scene threw their roof after them, barely missing them as they ran.

"What are you *doing?*" Conor said. "The Apotho-whatever is the bad guy!"

Is he? asked the real monster behind him.

There was a crash as the second monster knocked down the parsonage's front wall.

"Of course he is!" Conor shouted. "He refused to help heal the parson's daughters! And they *died!*"

The parson refused to believe the Apothecary could help, said the monster. *When times were easy, the parson nearly destroyed the Apothecary, but when the going grew tough, he was willing to throw aside his every belief if it would save his daughters.*

"So?" Conor said. "So would anyone! So would *everyone*! What did you *expect* him to do?"

I expected him to give the Apothecary the yew tree when the Apothecary first asked.

This stopped Conor. There were further crashes from the parsonage as another wall fell. "You'd have let yourself be killed?"

I am far more than just one tree, the monster said. *But yes, I would have let the yew tree be chopped down. It would have saved the parson's daughters. And many, many others besides.*

"But it would have killed the tree and made him rich!" Conor yelled. "He was evil!"

*He was greedy and rude and bitter, but he was still a healer. The parson, though, what was he? He was **nothing**. Belief is half of all healing. Belief in the cure, belief in the future that awaits. And here was a man who **lived** on belief, but who sacrificed it at the first challenge, right when he needed it most. He believed selfishly and fearfully. And it took the lives of his daughters.*

Conor grew angrier. "You said this was a story without tricks."

I said this was the story of a man punished for his selfishness. And so it is.

Seething, Conor looked again at the second monster destroying the parsonage. A giant monstrous leg knocked over a staircase with one kick. A giant monstrous arm swung back and demolished the walls to the parson's bedrooms.

Tell me, Conor O'Malley, the monster behind him asked. *Would you like to join in?*

"Join in?" Conor said, surprised.

It is most satisfying, I assure you.

The monster stepped forward, joining its second self, and put a giant foot through a settee not unlike Conor's grandma's. The monster looked back at Conor, waiting.

What shall I destroy next? it asked, stepping over to the second monster, and in a terrible blurring of the eyes, they merged together, making a single monster who was even bigger.

I await your command, boy, it said.

Conor could feel his breathing growing heavy again. His heart was racing and that feverish feeling had come over him once more. He waited a long moment.

Then he said, "Knock over the fireplace."

The monster's fist immediately lashed out and struck the stone hearth from its foundations, the brick chimney tumbling down on top of it in a loud clatter.

Conor's breath got heavier still, like he was the one doing the destroying.

"Throw away their beds," he said.

The monster picked up the beds from the two roofless bedrooms and flung them into the air, so hard they seemed to sail nearly to the horizon before crashing to the ground.

"Smash their furniture!" Conor shouted. "Smash everything!"

The monster stomped around the interior of the house, crushing every piece of furniture it could find with satisfying crashes and crunches.

"TEAR THE WHOLE THING DOWN!" Conor roared, and the monster roared in return and pounded at the remaining walls, knocking them to the ground. Conor rushed in to help, picking up a fallen branch and smashing through the windows that hadn't already been broken.

He was yelling as he did it, so loud he couldn't hear himself think, disappearing into the frenzy of destruction, just mindlessly smashing and smashing and smashing.

The monster was right. It was *very* satisfying.

Conor screamed until he was hoarse, smashed until his arms were sore, roared until he was nearly falling down with exhaustion. When he finally stopped, he found the monster watching him quietly from outside the wreckage. Conor panted and leaned on the branch to keep himself balanced.

*Now **that**,* said the monster, *is how destruction is properly done.*

And suddenly they were back in Conor's grandma's sitting room.

Conor saw that he had destroyed almost every inch of it.

DESTRUCTION

The settee was shattered into pieces beyond counting. Every wooden leg was broken, the upholstery ripped to shreds, hunks of stuffing strewn across the floor, along with the remains of the clock, flung from the wall and broken to almost unrecognizable bits. So too were the lamps and both small tables that had sat at the ends of the settee, as well as the bookcase under the front window, every book of which was torn from cover to cover. Even the wallpaper had been ripped back in dirty, uneven strips. The only thing left standing was the display cabinet, though its glass doors were smashed and everything inside hurled to the floor.

Conor stood there in shock. He looked down at his hands, which were covered in scratches and blood, his fingernails torn and ragged, aching from the labor.

"Oh, my God," he whispered.

He turned around to face the monster.

Which was no longer there.

"What did you *do*?" he shouted into the suddenly too quiet emptiness. He could barely move his feet from all the destroyed rubbish on the floor.

There was no *way* he could have done all this himself.

No way.

(. . . was there?)

"Oh, my God," he said again. "Oh, my God."

Destruction is very satisfying, he heard, but it was like a voice on the breeze, almost not there at all.

And then he heard his grandma's car pull into the driveway.

There was nowhere to run. No time to even get out of the back door and go off on his own somehow, somewhere she'd never find him.

But, he thought, not even his father would take him now when he found out what he had done. They'd never allow a boy who could do all this to go and live in a house with a baby—

"Oh, my God," Conor said again, his heart beating nearly out of his chest.

His grandma put her key in the lock and opened the front door.

In the split second after she came around the corner to the sitting room, still fiddling with her handbag, before she registered where Conor was or what had happened, he saw her face, how tired it

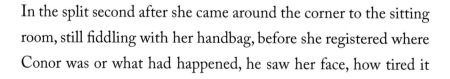

was, no news on it, good or bad, just the same old night at the hospital with Conor's mum, the same old night that was wearing them both so thin.

Then she looked up.

"What the–?" she said, stopping herself by reflex from saying *hell* in front of Conor. She froze, still holding her handbag in midair. Only her eyes moved, taking in the destruction of the sitting room in disbelief, almost refusing to see what was really there. Conor couldn't even hear her breathing.

And then she looked at him, her mouth open, her eyes open wide, too. She saw him standing there in the middle of it, his hands bloodied with his work.

Her mouth closed, but it didn't close into its usual hard shape. It trembled and shook, as if she was fighting back tears, as if she could barely hold the rest of her face together.

And then she groaned, deep in her chest, her mouth still closed.

It was a sound so painful, Conor could barely keep himself from putting his hands over his ears.

She made it again. And again. And then again until it became a single sound, a single ongoing horrible groan. Her handbag fell to the floor. She put her palms over her mouth as if that was all that would hold back the horrible, groaning, moaning, *keening* sound flooding out of her.

"Grandma?" Conor said, his voice high and tight with terror.

And then she screamed.

She took away her hands, balling them into fists, opened her mouth wide and screamed. Screamed so loudly that Conor *did* put his hands up to his ears. She wasn't looking at him, she wasn't looking at *anything*, just screaming into the air.

Conor had never been so frightened in all his life. It was like standing at the end of the world, almost like being alive and awake in his nightmare, the screaming, the *emptiness*—

Then she stepped into the room.

She kicked forward through the rubbish almost as if she didn't even see it. Conor backed away from her quickly, stumbling over the ruins of the settee. He kept a hand up to protect himself, expecting blows to land any moment—

But she wasn't coming for him.

She walked right past him, her face twisted in tears, the moaning spilling out of her again. She went to the display cabinet, the only thing remaining upright in the room.

And she grabbed it by one side—

And pulled on it hard once—

Twice—

And a third time.

Sending it crashing to the floor with a final-sounding *crunch*.

She gave a last moan and leaned forward to put her hands on her knees, her breath coming in ragged gasps.

She didn't look at Conor, didn't look at him once as she stood back up and left the room, leaving her handbag where she'd dropped it, going straight up to her bedroom and quietly shutting the door.

Conor stood there for a while, not knowing whether he should move or not.

After what seemed like forever, he went into his grandma's kitchen to get some empty trash bags. He worked on the mess late into the night, but there was just too much of it. Dawn was breaking by the time he finally gave up.

He climbed the stairs, not even bothering to wash off the dirt and dried blood. As he passed his grandma's room, he saw from the light under her door that she was still awake.

He could hear her in there, weeping.

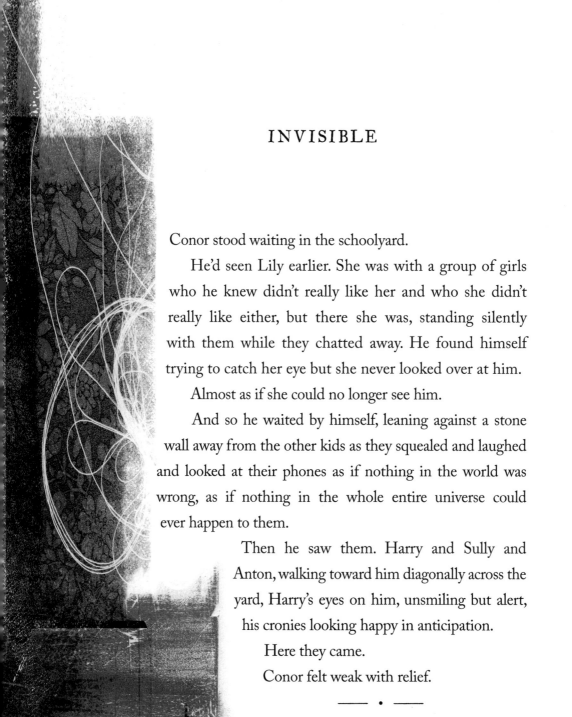

INVISIBLE

Conor stood waiting in the schoolyard.

He'd seen Lily earlier. She was with a group of girls who he knew didn't really like her and who she didn't really like either, but there she was, standing silently with them while they chatted away. He found himself trying to catch her eye but she never looked over at him.

Almost as if she could no longer see him.

And so he waited by himself, leaning against a stone wall away from the other kids as they squealed and laughed and looked at their phones as if nothing in the world was wrong, as if nothing in the whole entire universe could ever happen to them.

Then he saw them. Harry and Sully and Anton, walking toward him diagonally across the yard, Harry's eyes on him, unsmiling but alert, his cronies looking happy in anticipation.

Here they came.

Conor felt weak with relief.

—— • ——

He'd only slept long enough that morning to have the nightmare, as if things hadn't been bad enough. There he'd been again, with the horror and the falling, with the terrible, terrible thing that happened at the end. He'd woken up screaming. To a day that hardly seemed any better.

When he'd finally worked up the courage to go downstairs, his father was there in his grandma's kitchen, making breakfast.

His grandma was nowhere to be seen.

"Scrambled?" his father asked, holding up the pan where the eggs were cooking.

Conor nodded, even though he wasn't remotely hungry, and sat in a chair at the table. His father finished the eggs and put them on some buttered toast he'd also made, setting down two plates, one for Conor, one for himself. They sat and they ate.

The silence grew so heavy, Conor started to have difficulty breathing.

"That's quite a mess you made," his father finally said.

Conor continued to eat, taking the smallest bites of egg possible.

"She called me this morning. Very, very early."

Conor took another microscopic bite.

"Your mum's taken a turn, Con," his father said. Conor looked up quickly. "Your grandma's gone to the hospital now to talk to the doctors," his father continued. "I'm going to drop you off at school—"

"*School?*" Conor said. "I want to see Mum!"

But his father was already shaking his head. "It's no place for a kid right now. I'll drop you off at school and go to the hospital, but I'll pick you up right after and take you to her." His father looked down at his plate. "I'll pick you up sooner if . . . if I need to."

Conor set down his knife and fork. He didn't feel like eating anymore. Or maybe ever again.

"Hey," his father said. "Remember what I said about needing you to be brave? Well, now's the time you're going to have to do it, son." He nodded toward the sitting room. "I can see how much this is upsetting you." He gave a sad smile, which quickly disappeared. "So can your grandma."

"I didn't mean to," Conor said, his heart starting to thump. "I don't know what happened."

"It's okay," his father said.

Conor frowned. "It's *okay*?"

"Don't worry about it," his father said, going back to his breakfast. "Worse things happen at sea."

"What does that mean?"

"It means we're going to pretend like it never happened," his father said, firmly, "because other things are going on right now."

"Other things like Mum?"

His father sighed. "Finish your breakfast."

"You're not even going to punish me?"

"What would be the point, Con?" his father said, shaking his head. "What could possibly be the point?"

Conor hadn't heard a word of his lessons in school, but the teachers hadn't told him off for his inattentiveness, skipping over him when they asked questions to the class. Mrs. Marl didn't even make him hand in his Life Writing homework, even though it was due that day. Conor hadn't written a single sentence.

Not that it seemed to matter.

His classmates kept their distance from him, too, like he was giving off a bad smell. He tried to remember if he'd talked to any of them since he'd arrived this morning. He didn't think he had. Which meant he hadn't actually spoken to *anyone* since his father that morning.

How could something like that happen?

But, finally, here was Harry. And that, at least, felt normal.

"Conor O'Malley," Harry said, stopping a pace away from him. Sully and Anton hung back, sniggering.

Conor stood up from the wall, dropping his hands to his sides, preparing himself for wherever the punch might fall.

Except it didn't.

Harry just stood there. Sully and Anton stood there, too, their smiles slowly shrinking.

"What are you waiting for?" Conor asked.

"Yeah," Sully said to Harry, "what are you waiting for?"

"Hit him," Anton said.

Harry didn't move, his eyes still firmly locked on Conor.

Conor could only look back until it felt like there was nothing in the world except him and Harry. His palms were sweating. His heart was racing.

Just do it, he thought, and then realized he was saying it out loud. "Just do it!"

"Do what?" Harry said, calmly. "What on earth could you possibly want me to do, O'Malley?"

"He wants you to beat him into the ground," Sully said.

"He wants you to kick his arse," Anton said.

"Is that right?" Harry asked, seeming genuinely curious. "Is that really what you want?"

Conor said nothing, just stood there, fists clenched.

Waiting.

And then the bell went, ringing loudly, and Miss Kwan began to cross the yard at that moment, too, talking to another teacher, but eyeing the pupils around her, keeping a close watch in particular on Conor and Harry.

"I guess we'll never find out," Harry said, "what it is O'Malley wants."

Anton and Sully laughed, though it was clear they didn't get the joke, and all three started to make their way back inside.

But Harry watched Conor as they left, never looking away from him.

As he left Conor standing there alone.

Like he was completely invisible to the rest of the world.

YEW TREES

"Hey there, darling," his mum said, pushing herself up a bit in her bed as Conor came through the door.

He could see how much she struggled to do it.

"I'll just be out here," his grandma said, getting up from her seat and walking past without looking at him.

"I'm going to grab something from the vending machine, sport," his father said from the doorway. "Do you want anything?"

"I want you to stop calling me *sport*," Conor said, not taking his eyes off his mother.

Who laughed.

"Back in a bit," his father said, and left him alone with her.

"Come here," she said, patting the bed beside her. He went over and sat down next to her, taking care not to disturb either the tube they had stuck in her arm or the tube sending air down her nostrils or the tube he knew occasionally got taped to her chest, when the bright orange chemicals were pumped into her at her treatments.

"How's my Conor then?" she asked, reaching up a thin hand to brush his hair. He could see a yellow stain on her arm around where the tube went in and little purple bruises all the way along the inside of her elbow.

But she was smiling. It was tired, it was exhausted, but it was a smile.

"I know I must look a fright," she said.

"No, you don't," Conor said.

She brushed his hair again with her fingers. "I think I can forgive a kind lie."

"Are you okay?" Conor asked, and even though the question was in one sense completely ridiculous, she knew what he meant.

"Well, sweetheart," she said, "a couple of different things they've tried haven't worked like they wanted them to. And they've *not* worked a lot sooner than they were hoping they wouldn't. If that makes any sense."

Conor shook his head.

"No, not to me either, really," she said. He saw her smile get tighter, harder for her to hold. She took in a deep breath, and it ratcheted slightly as it went in, like there was something heavy in her chest.

"Things are going a little faster than I'd hoped, sweetheart," she said, and her voice was thick, thick in a way that made Conor's stomach twist even harder. He was suddenly glad he hadn't eaten since breakfast.

"*But,*" his mum said, voice still thick but smiling again.

"There's one more thing they're going to try, a medicine that's had some good results."

"Why didn't they try it before?" Conor asked.

"Remember all my treatments?" she said. "Losing my hair and all that throwing up?"

"Of course."

"Well, this is something you take when that hasn't worked how they wanted it to," she said. "It was always a possibility, but they were hoping not to have to use it at all." She looked down. "And they were hoping not to have to use it this soon."

"Does that mean it's too late?" Conor asked, setting the words free before he even knew what he was saying.

"No, Conor," she answered him, quickly. "Don't think that. It's not too late. It's never too late."

"Are you sure?"

She smiled again. "I believe every word I say," she said, her voice a little stronger.

Conor remembered what the monster had said. *Belief is half of healing.*

He still felt like he wasn't breathing, but the tension started to ebb a little, letting go of his stomach. His mum saw him relax a bit, and she started rubbing the skin on his arm.

"And here's something really interesting," she said, her voice sounding a bit more chipper. "You remember that tree on the hill behind our house?"

Conor's eyes went wide.

"Well, if you can believe it," his mum continued, not noticing, "this drug is actually *made* from yew trees."

"Yew trees?" Conor asked, his voice quiet.

"Yeah," his mum said. "I read about it way back, when this all started." She coughed into her hand, then coughed again. "I mean, I hoped it would never get this far, but it just seemed incredible that all that time we could see a yew tree from our own house. And that very tree could be the thing that healed me."

Conor's mind was whirling so fast it almost made him dizzy.

"The green things of this world are just wondrous, aren't they?" his mother went on. "We work so hard to get rid of them when sometimes they're the very thing that saves us."

"Is it going to save *you?*" Conor asked, barely able to even say it.

His mum smiled again. "I hope so," she said. "I believe so."

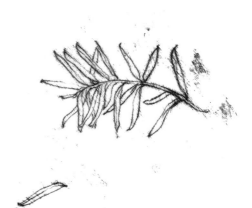

COULD IT BE?

Conor went out into the hospital corridor, his thoughts racing. Medicine made from yew trees. Medicine that could properly heal. Medicine just like the Apothecary refused to make for the parson. Though, to be honest, Conor was still a little unclear about why it was the parson's house that got knocked down.

Unless.

Unless the monster *was* here for a reason. Unless it had come walking to heal Conor's mother.

He hardly dared hope. He hardly dared *think* it.

No.

No, of course not. It couldn't be true, he was being stupid. The monster was a dream. That's all it was, a *dream*.

But the leaves. And the berries. And the sapling growing in the floor. And the destruction of his grandma's sitting room.

Conor felt suddenly light, like he was somehow starting to *float* in the air.

Could it be? Could it really be?

He heard voices and looked down the corridor. His dad and his grandma were fighting.

He couldn't hear what they were saying, but his grandma was pretty ferociously jabbing her finger toward his dad's chest. "Well, what do you want me to *do*?" his father said, loud enough to attract the attention of people passing in the corridor. Conor couldn't hear his grandma's response, but she came storming back down the corridor past Conor, still not looking at him as she went into his mother's room.

His father walked up shortly after, his shoulders slumped.

"What's going on?" Conor asked.

"Ah, your grandma's mad at me," his dad said, giving a quick smile. "Nothing new there."

"Why?"

His father made a face. "I've got some bad news, Conor," he said. "I have to fly back home tonight."

"Tonight?" Conor asked. *"Why?"*

"The baby's sick."

"Oh," Conor said. "What's wrong with her?"

"Probably nothing serious, but Stephanie's gone a bit crazy and taken her to the hospital and wants me to come back right now."

"And you're going?"

"I am but I'm coming back," his father said. "On Sunday after next, so it's not even two weeks. They've given me more time off work to come back and see you."

"Two weeks," Conor said, almost to himself. "But that's okay, though. Mum's on this new medicine, which is going to make her better. So by the time you get back—"

He stopped when he saw his father's face.

"Why don't we go for a walk, son?" his father asked.

There was a small park across from the hospital with paths among the trees. As Conor and his father walked through it toward an empty bench, they kept passing patients in hospital gowns, walking with their families or out on their own sneaking cigarettes. It made the park feel like an outdoor hospital room. Or a place where ghosts went to have a break.

"This is a talk, isn't it?" Conor said, as they sat down. "Everybody always wants to *have a talk* lately."

"Conor," his father said. "This new medicine your mum's taking—"

"It's going to make her well," Conor said, firmly.

His father paused for a moment. "No, Conor," he said. "It probably isn't."

"Yes, it is," Conor insisted.

"It's a last ditch effort, son. I'm sorry, but things have moved too fast."

"It'll heal her. I know it will."

"Conor," his father said. "The other reason your grandma was mad at me was because she doesn't think me or your mum have been honest enough with you. About what's really happening."

"What does Grandma know about it?"

Conor's father put a hand on his shoulder. "Conor, your mum—"

"She's going to be okay," Conor said, shaking it off and standing up. "This new medicine is the secret. It's the whole reason why. I'm telling you, I know."

His father looked confused. "Reason for what?"

"So you just go back to America," Conor carried on, "and go back to your other family and we'll be fine here without you. Because this is going to work."

"Conor, no—"

"Yes, it *is*. It's going to work."

"Son," his father said, leaning forward. "Stories don't always have happy endings."

This stopped him. Because they didn't, did they? That's one thing the monster had definitely taught him. Stories were wild, wild animals and went off in directions you couldn't expect.

His father was shaking his head. "This is too much to ask of you. It is, I know it is. It's unfair and cruel and not how things should be."

Conor didn't answer.

"I'll be back a week from Sunday," his father said. "Just keep that in mind, okay?"

Conor blinked up into the sun. It really had been an incredibly warm October, like the summer was still fighting to stick around.

"How long will you stay?" Conor finally asked.

"For as long as I can."

"And then you'll go back."

"I have to. I've got—"

"Another family there," Conor finished.

His father tried to reach out a hand again, but Conor was already heading back toward the hospital.

Because no, it *would* work, it *would,* that was the whole reason the monster had come walking. It *had* to be. If the monster was real at all then that *had* to be the reason.

Conor looked at the clock on the front of the hospital as he went back inside.

Eight more hours until 12:07.

NO TALE

"Can you heal her?" Conor asked.

The yew is a healing tree, the monster said.
It is the form I choose most to walk in.

Conor frowned. "That's not really an answer."

The monster just gave him that evil grin.

Conor's grandma had driven him back to her house when his mum had fallen asleep after not eating her dinner. His grandma still hadn't spoken to him about the destruction of her sitting room. She'd barely spoken to him *at all*.

"I'm going back," she said, as he got out of the car. "Fix yourself something to eat. I know you can at least do that."

"Do you think Dad's at the airport by now?" Conor asked.

All his grandma did in response was sigh impatiently. He shut the door, and she drove away. After he'd gone inside, the clock—the cheap, battery-operated one in the kitchen, which was all they had now—crept toward midnight without her returning or calling. He thought about calling her himself, but she'd already yelled at him once when her ringtone had woken up his mum.

It didn't matter. In fact, it made it easier. He hadn't had to pretend to go to bed. He'd waited until the clock read 12:07. Then he went outside and said, "Where are you?"

And the monster said, *I am here* and stepped over his grandma's office shed in one easy motion.

"Can you *heal* her?" Conor asked again, more firmly.

The monster looked down at him. *It is not up to me.*

"Why not?" Conor asked. "You tear down houses and rescue witches. You say every bit of you can heal if only people would use it."

If your mother can be healed, the monster said, *then the yew tree will do it.*

Conor crossed his arms. "Is that a yes?"

Then the monster did something it hadn't done until now.

It sat down.

It placed its entire great weight on top of his grandma's office. Conor could hear the wood groan and saw the roof sag. His heart leapt in his throat. If he destroyed her office, too, there's no telling what she'd do to him. Probably ship him off to prison. Or worse, boarding school.

You still do not know why you called me, do you? the monster asked. *You still do not know why I have come walking. It is not as if I do this every day, Conor O'Malley.*

"I didn't call you," Conor said. "Unless it was in a dream or something. And even if I did, it was obviously for my mum."

Was it?

"Well, why else?" Conor said, his voice rising. "It wasn't just to hear terrible stories that make no sense."

Are you forgetting your grandmother's sitting room?

Conor couldn't quite suppress a small smile.

As I thought, said the monster.

"I'm being serious," Conor said.

*So am I. But we are not yet ready for the third and final story. That will be soon. And after that you will tell me **your** story, Conor O'Malley. You will tell me your truth.* The monster leaned forward. *And you know of what I speak.*

The mist surrounded them again suddenly, and his grandma's yard faded away. The world changed to gray and emptiness, and Conor knew exactly where he was, exactly what the world had changed into.

He was inside the nightmare.

—— • ——

This is what it felt like, this is what it *looked* like, the edges of the world crumbling away and Conor holding on to her hands, feeling them slip from his grasp, feeling her *fall*–

"No!" he cried out. "No! Not this!"

The mist retreated and he was back in his grandma's yard again, the monster still sitting on her office roof.

"That's not my truth," Conor said, his voice shaking. "That's just a nightmare."

Nevertheless, the monster said, standing, the roof beams of his grandma's office seeming to sigh with relief, *that is what will happen after the third tale.*

"Great," Conor said. "Another story when there are more important things going on."

Stories are important, the monster said. *They can be more important than anything. If they carry the truth.*

"Life writing," Conor said, sourly, under his breath.

The monster looked surprised. *Indeed,* it said. It turned to go, but glanced back at Conor. *Look for me soon.*

"I want to know what's going to happen with my mum," Conor said.

The monster paused. *Do you not know already?*

"You said you were a tree of healing," Conor said. "Well, I need you to *heal*!"

And so I shall, the monster said.

And with a gust of wind, it was gone.

I NO LONGER SEE YOU

"I want to go to the hospital, too," Conor said the next morning in the car with his grandma. "I don't want to go to school today."

His grandma just drove. It was quite possible she was never going to speak to him again.

"How was she last night?" he asked. He'd waited up for a long time after the monster left, but had still fallen asleep before his grandma came back.

"Much the same," she said, tersely, keeping her eyes firmly on the road.

"Is the new medicine helping?"

She didn't answer this one for so long, he thought she wasn't going to and was on the verge of asking again when she said, "It's too soon to tell."

Conor let a few streets go by, then he asked, "When is she going to come home?"

This one his grandma didn't answer, even though it was another half hour before they got to school.

—— • ——

There was no hope of paying attention in lessons. Which, once again, didn't matter because none of the teachers asked him a question anyway. Neither did his classmates. By the time lunch break came around, he'd passed another morning not having said a word to anyone.

He sat alone at the far edge of the dining hall, his food uneaten in front of him. The room was unbelievably loud, roaring with the sounds of his classmates and all their screaming and yelling and fighting and laughing. Conor did his best to ignore it.

The monster would heal her. Of course it would. Why *else* would it have come? There was no other explanation. It had come walking as a tree of healing, the same tree that made the medicine for his mother, so why else?

Please, Conor thought as he stared at his still full lunch tray. *Please.*

Two hands slapped down hard on either side of the tray from across the table, knocking Conor's orange juice into his lap.

Conor stood up, though not quickly enough. His trousers were soaked in liquid, dripping down his legs.

"O'Malley's wet himself!" Sully was already shouting, with Anton cracking up beside him.

"Here!" Anton said, flicking some of the puddle from the table at Conor. "You missed some!"

Harry stood between Anton and Sully, as ever, his arms crossed, staring.

Conor stared back.

Neither of them moved for so long that Sully and Anton quieted down. They started to look uncomfortable as the staring contest continued, wondering what Harry was going to do next.

Conor wondered, too.

"I think I've worked you out, O'Malley," Harry finally said. "I think I know what it is you're asking for."

"You're gonna get it now," Sully said. He and Anton laughed, bumping fists.

Conor couldn't see any teachers out of the corner of his eye, so he knew Harry had chosen a moment when they could bother him unseen.

Conor was on his own.

Harry stepped forward, still calm.

"Here is the hardest hit of all, O'Malley," Harry said. "Here is the very worst thing I can do to you."

He held out his hand, as if asking for a handshake.

He *was* asking for a handshake.

Conor responded almost automatically, putting out his own hand and shaking Harry's before he even thought about what he was doing. They shook hands like two businessmen at the end of a meeting.

"Good-bye, O'Malley," Harry said, looking into Conor's eyes. "I no longer see you."

Then he let go of Conor's hand, turned his back, and walked away. Anton and Sully looked even more confused, but after a second, they walked away, too.

None of them looked back at Conor.

There was a huge digital clock on the wall of the dining hall, bought sometime in the seventies as the latest in technology and never replaced, even though it was older than Conor's mum. As Conor watched Harry walk away, walk away without looking back, walk away without doing *anything*, Harry moved past the digital clock.

Lunch started at 11:55 and ended at 12:40.

The clock currently read 12:06.

Harry's words echoed in Conor's head.

"I no longer see you."

Harry kept walking away, keeping good on his promise.

"I no longer see you."

The clock ticked over to 12:07.

It is time for the third tale, the monster said from behind him.

THE THIRD TALE

There was once an invisible man, the monster continued, though Conor kept his eyes firmly on Harry, *who had grown tired of being unseen.*

Conor set himself into a walk.

A walk after Harry.

*It was not that he was **actually** invisible,* the monster said, following Conor, the room volume dropping as they passed. *It was that people had become used to not seeing him.*

"Hey!" Conor called. Harry didn't turn round. Neither did Sully nor Anton, though they were still sniggering as Conor picked up his pace.

And if no one sees you, the monster said, picking up its pace, too, *are you really there at all?*

"HEY!" Conor called loudly.

The dining hall had fallen silent now, as Conor and the monster moved faster after Harry.

Harry who had still not turned around.

Conor reached him and grabbed him by the shoulder, twisting him around. Harry pretended to question what had

happened, looking hard at Sully, acting like he was the one who'd done it. "Quit messing about," Harry said and turned away again.

Turned away from Conor.

And then one day the invisible man decided, the monster said, its voice ringing in Conor's ears, *I will **make** them see me.*

"How?" Conor asked, breathing heavily again, not turning back to see the monster standing there, not looking at the reaction of the room to the huge monster now in their midst, though he was aware of nervous murmurs and a strange anticipation in the air. "How did the man do it?"

Conor could feel the monster close behind him, knew that it was kneeling, knew that it was putting its face up to his ear to whisper into it, to tell him the rest of the story.

He called, it said, *for a **monster.***

And it reached a huge, monstrous hand past Conor and knocked Harry flying across the floor.

Trays clattered and people screamed as Harry tumbled past them. Anton and Sully looked aghast, first at Harry, then back at Conor.

Their faces changed as they saw him. Conor took another step toward them, feeling the monster towering behind him.

Anton and Sully turned and ran.

"What do you think you're playing at, O'Malley?" Harry said as he pulled himself up from the floor, holding his forehead where he'd hit it as he fell. He took his hand away and a few people screamed as they saw blood.

Conor kept moving forward, people scrambling to get out of his way. The monster came with him, matching him step for step.

"You don't see me?" Conor shouted as he came. "You don't *see* me?"

"No, O'Malley!" Harry shouted back as he stood. "No, I don't. No one here does!"

Conor stopped and looked around slowly. The whole room was watching them now, waiting to see what would happen.

Except when Conor turned to face them. Then they looked away, like it was too embarrassing or painful to actually look at him directly. Only Lily held his eyes for longer than a second, her face anxious and hurt.

"You think this scares me, O'Malley?" Harry said, touching the blood on his forehead. "You think I'm ever going to be afraid of you?"

Conor said nothing, just started moving forward again.

Harry took a step back.

"Conor O'Malley," he said, his voice growing poisonous now. "Who everyone's sorry for because of his mum. Who swans around school acting like he's so different, like no one knows his *suffering*."

Conor kept walking. He was almost there.

"Conor O'Malley who wants to be punished," Harry said, still stepping back, his eyes on Conor's. "Conor O'Malley who *needs* to be punished. And why is that, Conor O'Malley? What secrets do you hide that are so terrible?"

"You *shut up*," Conor said.

And he heard the monster's voice say it with him.

Harry backed up another step until he was against a window. It felt like the whole school was holding its breath, waiting to see what Conor would do. He could hear a teacher or two calling from outside, finally noticing something was going on.

"But do you know what *I* see when I look at you, O'Malley?" Harry said.

Conor clenched his hands into fists.

Harry leaned forward, his eyes flashing. "I see *nothing*," he said.

Without turning around, Conor asked the monster a question.

"What did you do to help the invisible man?"

And he felt the monster's voice again, like it was in his own head.

I made them see, it said.

Conor clenched his fists even tighter.

Then the monster leapt forward to make Harry see.

PUNISHMENT

"I don't even know what to say." The headmistress made an exasperated sound and shook her head. "What can I possibly say to you, Conor?"

Conor kept his eyes on the carpet, which was the color of spilled wine. Miss Kwan was there, too, sitting behind him, as if he might try to escape. He sensed rather than saw the headmistress lean forward. She was older than Miss Kwan. And somehow twice as scary.

"You put him in the *hospital*, Conor," she said. "You broke his arm, his nose, and I'll bet his teeth are never going to look that pretty again. His parents are threatening to sue the school *and* file charges against you."

Conor looked up at that.

"They were a little hysterical, Conor," Miss Kwan said behind him, "and I don't blame them. I explained what's been going on, though. That he had been regularly bullying you and that your circumstances were . . . special."

Conor winced at the word.

"It was actually the bullying part that scared them off," Miss

Kwan said, scorn in her voice. "Doesn't look good to prospective universities these days, apparently, accusations of bullying."

"*But that's not the point!*" the headmistress said, so loud she made both Conor and Miss Kwan jump. "I can't even make sense of what actually happened." She looked at some papers on her desk, reports from teachers and other students, Conor guessed. "I'm not even sure how one boy could have caused so much damage by himself."

Conor had *felt* what the monster was doing to Harry, felt it in his own hands. When the monster gripped Harry's shirt, Conor felt the material against his own palms. When the monster struck a blow, Conor felt the sting of it in his own fist. When the monster held Harry's arm behind his back, Conor had felt Harry's muscles resisting.

Resisting, but not winning.

Because how could a boy beat a monster?

He remembered all the screaming and running. He remembered the other kids fleeing to get teachers. He remembered the circle around him opening wider and wider as the monster told the story of all that he'd done for the invisible man.

Never invisible again, the monster kept saying as he pummeled Harry. *Never invisible again.*

There came a point when Harry stopped trying to fight back,

when the blows from the monster were too strong, too many, too fast, when he began begging the monster to stop.

Never invisible again, the monster said, finally letting up, its huge branch-like fists curled tight as a clap of thunder.

It turned to Conor.

But there are harder things than being invisible, it said.

And it vanished, leaving Conor standing alone over the shivering, bleeding Harry.

Everyone in the dining hall was staring at Conor now. Everyone could see him, all eyes looking his way. There was silence in the room, too much silence for so many kids, and for a moment, before the teachers broke it up – where had they been? Had the monster kept them from seeing? Or had it really been so short an amount of time? – you could hear the wind rushing in an open window, a wind that dropped a few small, spiky leaves to the floor.

Then there were adult hands on Conor, dragging him away.

"What do you have to say for yourself?" the headmistress asked.

Conor shrugged.

"I'm going to need more than that," she said. "You seriously hurt him."

"It wasn't me," Conor mumbled.

"What was that?" she said sharply.

"It wasn't me," Conor said, more clearly. "It was the monster who did it."

"The monster," the headmistress said.

"I didn't even touch Harry."

The headmistress made a wedge shape with her fingertips and placed her elbows on her desk. She glanced at Miss Kwan.

"An entire dining hall saw you hitting Harry, Conor," Miss Kwan said. "They saw you knocking him down. They saw you pushing him over a table. They saw you banging his head against the floor." Miss Kwan leaned forward. "They heard you yelling about being seen. About not being invisible anymore."

Conor flexed his hands slowly. They were sore again. Just like after the destruction of his grandma's sitting room.

"I can understand how angry you must be," Miss Kwan said, her voice getting slightly softer. "I mean, we haven't even been able to reach any kind of parent or guardian for you."

"My dad flew back to America," Conor said. "And my grandma's started keeping her phone on silent so she won't wake up Mum." He scratched the back of his hand. "Grandma'll probably call you back, though."

The headmistress sat back heavily in her chair. "School rules dictate immediate expulsion," she said.

Conor felt his stomach sink, felt his whole body droop under a ton of extra weight.

But then he realized it was drooping because the weight had been *removed*.

Understanding flooded him, *relief* did, too, so powerful it almost made him cry, right there in the headmistress's office.

He was going to be punished. It was finally going to happen. Everything was going to make sense again. She was going to expel him.

Punishment was coming.

Thank God. Thank *God—*

"But how could I do that?" the headmistress said.

Conor froze.

"How could I do that and still call myself a teacher?" she said. "With all that you're going through." She frowned. "With all that we know about Harry." She shook her head slightly. "There will come a day when we'll talk about this, Conor O'Malley. And we *will*, believe me." She started gathering the papers on her desk. "But today is not that day." She gave him a last look. "You have bigger things to think about."

It took Conor a moment to realize it was over. That this was it. This was all he was going to get.

"You're not punishing me?" he said.

The headmistress gave him a grim smile, almost kind, and then she said almost exactly the same thing his father had said. "What purpose could that possibly serve?"

—— • ——

Miss Kwan walked him back to his class. The two pupils they passed in the corridor backed up against the wall to let him go by.

His classroom fell silent when he opened the door, and no one, including the teacher, said a word as he made his way back to his desk. Lily, at the desk beside him, looked like she was going to say something. But she didn't.

No one spoke to him for the rest of the day.

There are worse things than being invisible, the monster had said, and it was right.

Conor was no longer invisible. They all saw him now.

But he was further away than ever.

A NOTE

A few days passed. Then a few more. It was hard to tell exactly how many. They all seemed to be one big, gray day to Conor. He'd get up in the morning and his grandma wouldn't talk to him, not even about the phone call from the headmistress. He'd go to school, and no one would talk to him there either. He'd visit his mum in the hospital, and she'd be too tired to talk to him. His dad would phone, and he'd have nothing to say.

There was no sign of the monster either, not since the attack on Harry, even though it was supposed to be time for Conor to tell a story in return. Every night, Conor waited.

Every night, it didn't appear. Maybe because it knew Conor didn't know what story to tell. Or that Conor *did* know, but would refuse.

Eventually, Conor would fall asleep, and the nightmare would come. It came every time he slept now, and worse than before, if that was possible. He'd wake up shouting three or four times a night, once so bad his grandma knocked on his door to see if he was all right.

She didn't come in, though.

The weekend arrived and was spent at the hospital, though his mum's new medicine was taking its time to work and meanwhile she had developed an infection in her lungs. Her pain had gotten worse, too, so she spent most of the time either asleep or not making a lot of sense because of the painkillers. Conor's grandma would send him out when she was like that, and he got so familiar with wandering around the hospital he once correctly took a lost old woman to the X-ray department.

Lily and her mum came to visit on the weekend, too, but he made sure he spent the whole time they were there reading magazines in the gift shop.

Then, somehow, he was back at school again. As incredible as it seemed, time kept moving forward for the rest of the world.

The rest of the world that wasn't waiting.

Mrs. Marl was handing back the Life Writing homework. To everyone who *had* a life, anyway. Conor just sat at his desk, chin in hand, looking at the clock. It was still two and a half hours until 12:07. Not that it would probably matter. He was beginning to think the monster was gone for good.

Someone else who wouldn't talk to him, then.

"Hey," he heard, whispered in his general vicinity. Making fun of him no doubt. Look at Conor O'Malley, just sitting there like a lump. What a freak.

"Hey," he heard again, this time more insistent.

He realized it was someone whispering to *him*.

Lily was sitting across the aisle, where she'd sat throughout all the years they'd been in school together. She kept looking up at Mrs. Marl, but her fingers were slyly holding out a note.

A note for Conor.

"Take it," she whispered out of the side of her mouth, gesturing with the note.

Conor looked to see if Mrs. Marl was watching, but she was too busy expressing mild disappointment that Sully's life had an awfully close resemblance to a particular insect-based superhero. Conor reached across the aisle and took the note.

It was folded what seemed like a couple of hundred times, and getting it open was like untying a knot. He gave Lily an irritated look, but she was still pretending to watch the teacher.

Conor flattened the note on his desk and read it. For all the folding, it was only four lines long.

Four lines, and the world went quiet.

—— • ——

I'm sorry for telling everyone about your mum, read the first line.

I miss being your friend, read the second.

Are you okay? read the third.

I see you, read the fourth, with the *I* underlined about a hundred times.

He read it again. And again.

He looked back over to Lily, who was busy receiving all kinds of praise from Mrs. Marl, but he could see that she was blushing furiously, and not just because of what Mrs. Marl was saying.

Mrs. Marl moved on, passing lightly over Conor.

When she was gone, Lily looked at him. Looked him right in the eye.

And she was right. She saw him, really *saw* him.

He had to swallow before he could speak.

"Lily–" he started to say, but the door to the classroom opened and the school secretary entered, beckoning to Mrs. Marl and whispering something to her.

They both turned to look at Conor.

100 YEARS

Conor's grandma stopped outside his mum's hospital room.

"Aren't you coming in?" Conor asked.

She shook her head. "I'll be down in the waiting room," she said, and left him to enter on his own.

He had a sour feeling in his stomach at what he might find inside. They'd never pulled him out of school before, not in the middle of the day, not even when she was hospitalized last Easter.

Questions raced through his mind.

Questions he ignored.

He pushed open the door, fearing the worst.

But his mum was awake, her bed in its sitting-up position. What's more, she was smiling, and for a second, Conor's heart leapt. The treatment must have worked. The yew tree had healed her. The monster had done it—

Then he saw that the smile didn't match her eyes. She was happy to see him, but she was frightened, too. And sad. And more tired than he'd ever seen her, which was saying something.

And they wouldn't have pulled him out of school to tell him she was feeling a little bit better.

"Hi, son," she said, and when she said it, her eyes filled and he could hear the thickness in her voice.

Conor could feel himself slowly starting to get very, very angry.

"Come here," she said, tapping the bedcovers next to her.

He didn't sit there, though, slumping instead in a chair next to her bed.

"How're you doing, sweetheart?" she asked, her voice faint, her breath even shakier than it had been yesterday. There seemed to be more tubes invading her today, giving her medicines and air and who knew what else? She wasn't wearing a scarf, and her head was bare and white in the room's fluorescent lights. Conor felt an almost irresistible urge to find something to cover it, protect it, before anyone saw how vulnerable it was.

"What's going on?" he asked. "Why did Grandma get me out of school?"

"I wanted to *see* you," she said, "and the way the morphine's been sending me off to Cloud Cuckoo Land, I didn't know if I'd have the chance later."

Conor crossed his arms tightly in front of himself. "You're awake in the evenings sometimes," he said. "You could have seen me tonight."

He knew he was asking a question. He knew she knew it, too.

And so he knew when she spoke again that she was giving him an answer.

"I wanted to see you *now,* Conor," she said, and again her voice was thick and her eyes were wet.

"This is the talk, isn't it?" Conor said, far more sharply than he'd wanted to. "This is . . ."

He didn't finish the sentence.

"Look at me, son," she said, because he'd been staring at the floor. Slowly, he looked back up to her. She was giving the super-tired smile, and he saw how deeply pressed into her pillows she was, like she didn't even have the strength to raise her head. He realized that they'd raised the bed because she wouldn't have been able to look at him otherwise.

She took a deep breath to speak, which set her off into a terrible, heavy-sounding coughing fit. It took a few long moments before she could finally talk again.

"I spoke to the doctor this morning," she said, her voice weak. "The new treatment isn't working, Conor."

"The one from the yew tree?"

"Yes."

Conor frowned. "How can it not be working?"

His mum swallowed. "Things have moved just too fast. It was a faint hope. And now there's this infection–"

"But how can it not be *working?*" Conor said again, almost like he was asking someone else.

"I know," his mum said, her sad smile still there. "Looking at that yew tree every day, it felt like I had a friend out there who'd help me if things got to their worst."

Conor still had his arms crossed. "But it *didn't* help."

His mum shook her head slightly. She had a worried look on her face, and Conor understood that she was worried about *him*.

"So what happens now?" Conor asked. "What's the next treatment?"

She didn't answer. Which was an answer in itself.

Conor said it out loud anyway. "There aren't any more treatments."

"I'm sorry, son," his mum said, tears sneaking out of her eyes now, even though she kept up her smile. "I've never been more sorry about anything in my life."

Conor looked at the floor again. He felt like he couldn't breathe, like the nightmare was squeezing the breath right out of him. "You said it would work," he said, his voice catching.

"I know."

"You *said*. You *believed* it would work."

"I know."

"You lied," Conor said, looking back up at her. "You've been lying this whole time."

"I *did* believe it would work," she said. "It's probably what's kept me here so long, Conor. Believing it so *you* would."

His mother reached for his hand, but he moved it away.

"You lied," he said again.

"I think, deep in your heart, you've always known," his mother said. "Haven't you?"

Conor didn't answer her.

"It's okay that you're angry, sweetheart," she said. "It really, really is." She gave a little laugh. "I'm pretty angry, too, to tell you the truth. But I want you to know this, Conor, it's important that you listen to me. Are you listening?"

She reached out for him again. After a second, he let her take his hand, but her grip was so weak, *so* weak.

"You be as angry as you need to be," she said. "Don't let anyone tell you otherwise. Not your grandma, not your dad, no one. And if you need to break things, then by God, you break them good and hard."

He couldn't look at her. He just *couldn't*.

"And if, one day," she said, really crying now, "you look back and you feel bad for being so angry, if you feel bad for being *so* angry at me that you couldn't even speak to me, then you have to know, Conor, you have to know that it was *okay*. It was okay. That I *knew*. I *know*, okay? I know everything you need to tell me without you having to say it out loud. All right?"

He still couldn't look at her. He couldn't raise his head, it felt so heavy. He was bent in two, like he was being torn right through his middle.

But he nodded.

He heard her sigh a long, wheezy breath, and he could hear the relief in it, as well as the exhaustion. "I'm sorry, son," she said. "I'm going to need more painkillers."

He let go of her hand. She reached over and pressed the button on the machine the hospital had given her, which administered painkillers so strong she was never able to stay awake after she took them. When she finished, she took his hand again.

"I wish I had a hundred years," she said, very quietly. "A hundred years I could give to you."

He didn't answer her. A few seconds later, the medicine had sent her to sleep, but it didn't matter.

They'd had the talk.

There was nothing more to say.

"Conor?" his grandma said, poking her head in the door sometime later, Conor didn't know how long.

"I want to go home," he said, quietly.

"Conor–"

"*My* home," he said, raising his head, his eyes red, with grief, with shame, with *anger*. "The one with the yew tree."

WHAT'S THE USE OF YOU?

"I'm going back to the hospital, Conor," his grandma said, dropping him off at his house. "I don't like leaving her like this. What do you need that's so important?"

"There's something I have to do," Conor said, looking at the home where he'd spent his entire life. It seemed empty and foreign, even though it wasn't very long since he'd left.

He realized it would probably never be his home again.

"I'll be back in an hour to get you," his grandma said. "We'll have dinner at the hospital."

Conor wasn't listening. He was already shutting the car door behind him.

"One hour," his grandma called to him through the closed door. "You're going to want to be there tonight."

Conor kept on walking up his own front steps.

"Conor?" his grandma called after him. But he didn't look back.

He barely heard her pull the car out onto the street and drive away.

—— • ——

Inside, the house smelled of dust and stale air. He didn't even bother shutting the door behind him. He headed straight through to the kitchen and looked out of the window.

There was the church on the rise. There was the yew tree standing guard over its cemetery.

Conor went out across his backyard. He hopped up on the garden table where his mum used to drink Pimm's in the summer, and he lifted himself up and over the back fence. He hadn't done this since he was a little, little kid, so long ago it had been his father who'd punished him for it. The break in the barbed wire by the railway line was still there, and he squeezed through, tearing his shirt, not caring.

He crossed the tracks, barely checking to see if a train was coming, climbed another fence, and found himself at the base of the hill leading up to the church. He hopped over the low stone wall that surrounded it and climbed up through the tombstones, all the while keeping the tree in his sights.

And all the while, it stayed a tree.

Conor began to run.

"Wake up!" he started shouting before he even reached it. "WAKE UP!"

He got to the trunk and started kicking it. "I said, *wake up*! I don't care what time it is!"

He kicked it again.

And harder.

And once more.

And the tree stepped out of the way, so quickly that Conor lost his balance and fell.

You will do yourself harm if you keep that up, the monster said, looming over him.

"It didn't work!" Conor shouted, getting to his feet. "You said the yew tree would heal her, but it didn't!"

I said if she could be healed, the yew tree would do it, the monster said. *It seems that she could not.*

Anger rose even higher in Conor's chest, thumping his heart against his rib cage. He attacked the monster's legs, battering the bark with his hands, bringing up bruises almost immediately. "Heal her! You have to heal her!"

Conor, the monster said.

"What's the *use* of you if you can't heal her?" Conor said, pounding away. "Just stupid stories and getting me into trouble and everyone looking at me like I've got a disease—"

He stopped because the monster had reached down a hand and plucked him into the air.

You are the one who called me, Conor O'Malley, it said, looking at him seriously. *You are the one with the answers to these questions.*

"If I called you," Conor said, his face boiling red, tears he

171

was hardly aware of streaming angrily down his cheeks, "it was to save her! It was to heal her!"

There was a rustling through the monster's leaves, like the wind stirring them in a long, slow sigh.

I did not come to heal her, the monster said. *I came to heal you.*

"Me?" Conor said, stopping his squirming in the monster's hand. "*I* don't need healing. My mum's the one who's . . ."

But he couldn't say it. Even now he couldn't say it. Even though they'd had the talk. Even though he'd known it all along. Because of *course* he had, of *course* he did, no matter how much he'd wanted to believe it wasn't true, of course he knew. But *still* he couldn't say it.

Couldn't say that she was–

He was still crying furiously and finding it hard to breathe. He felt like he was splitting open, like his body was twisting apart.

He looked back up at the monster. "Help me," he said, quietly.

It is time, the monster said, *for the fourth tale.*

Conor let out an angry yell. "No! That's not what I meant! There are more important things happening!"

Yes, the monster said. *Yes, there are.*

It opened its free hand.

The mist surrounded them again.

And once more, they were in the middle of the nightmare.

THE FOURTH TALE

Even held in the monster's huge, strong hand, Conor could feel the terror seeping into him, could feel the blackness of it all start to fill his lungs and choke them, could feel his stomach beginning to fall—

"No!" he shouted, squirming some more, but the monster held him tight. "No! Please!"

The hill, the church, the graveyard were all gone, even the sun had disappeared, leaving them in the middle of a cold darkness, one that had followed Conor ever since his mother had first been hospitalized, from before that when she'd started the treatments that made her lose her hair, from before that when she'd had a flu that didn't go away until she went to a doctor and it wasn't the flu at all, from before even *that* when she'd started to complain about how tired she was feeling, ever since before all that, ever since *forever,* it felt like, the nightmare had been there, stalking him, surrounding him, cutting him off, making him alone.

It felt like he'd never been anywhere else.

"Get me out of here!" he yelled. "Please!"

It is time, the monster said again, *for the fourth tale.*

"I don't know any tales!" Conor said, his mind lurching with fear.

If you do not tell it, the monster said, *I shall have to tell it for you.* It held Conor up closer to its face. *And believe me when I say, you do not want* **that***.*

"Please," Conor said again. "I have to get back to my mum."

But, the monster said, turning across the blackness, *she is already here.*

The monster set him down abruptly, almost dropping him to the earth, and Conor stumbled forward.

He recognized the cold ground under his hands, recognized the clearing he was in, bordered on three sides by a dark and impenetrable forest, recognized the fourth side, a cliff, flying off into even further blackness.

And on the cliff's edge, his mum.

She had her back to him, but she was looking over her shoulder, smiling. She looked as weak as she had in the hospital, but she gave him a small wave.

"Mum!" Conor yelled, feeling too heavy to stand, as he did every time the nightmare began. "You have to get out of here!"

His mum didn't move, though she looked a little worried at what he'd said.

Conor dragged himself forward, straining at the effort. "Mum, you have to run!"

"I'm fine, darling," she said. "There's nothing to worry about."

"Mum, run! Please, *run!*"

"But darling, there's—"

She stopped and turned back to the cliff's edge, as if she'd heard something.

"No," Conor whispered to himself. He pulled himself forward some more, but she was too far, too far to reach in time, and he felt so *heavy*—

There was a low sound from below the cliff. A rumbling, *booming* noise.

Like something big was moving down below.

Something bigger than the world.

And it was climbing up the cliff face.

"Conor?" his mum asked, looking back at him.

But Conor knew. It was too late.

The real monster was coming.

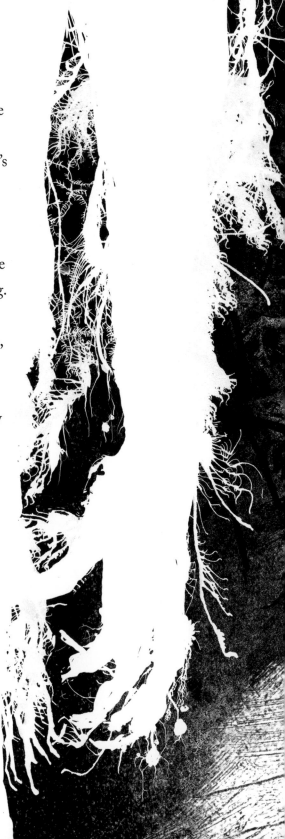

"Mum!" Conor shouted, forcing himself to his feet, pushing against the invisible weight pressing down on him. "MUM!"

"Conor!" his mum shouted, backing away from the cliff's edge.

But the booming was getting louder. And louder. And louder still.

"MUM!"

He knew he wouldn't get there in time.

Because with a roar, a cloud of burning darkness lifted two giant fists over the cliff top. They hovered in the air for a long moment, over his mum as she tried to scramble back.

But she was too weak, much too weak—

And the fists rushed down together in a violent pounce and grabbed her, pulling her over the edge of the cliff.

And at last, Conor could run.

With a shout, he broke across the clearing, running so fast he nearly toppled over, and he threw himself toward her, toward her out-reaching hands as the dark fists pulled her over the edge.

And his hands caught hers.

This was the nightmare. This was the nightmare that woke him up screaming every night. This was it happening, right now, right *here*.

He was on the cliff edge, bracing himself, holding on to his mother's hands with all his strength, trying to keep her from being pulled down into the blackness, pulled down by the creature below the cliff.

Who he could see all of now.

The *real* monster, the one he was properly afraid of, the one he'd expected to see when the yew tree first showed up, the real, nightmare monster, formed of cloud and ash and dark flames, but with real muscle, real strength, real red eyes that glared back at him and flashing teeth that would eat his mother alive. *I've seen worse*, Conor had told the yew tree that first night.

And here was the worse thing.

"Help me, Conor!" his mum yelled. "Don't let go!"

"I won't!" Conor yelled back. "I promise!"

The nightmare monster gave a roar and pulled harder, its fists straining around his mother's body.

179

And she began to slip from Conor's grasp.

"No!" he called.

His mum screamed in terror. "Please, Conor! Hold on to me!"

"I will!" Conor yelled. He turned back to the yew tree, standing there, not moving. "Help me! I can't hold on to her!"

But it just stood there, watching.

"Conor!" his mum yelled.

And her hands were slipping.

"Conor!" she yelled again.

"Mum!" he cried, gripping tighter.

But they were slipping from his grasp, and she was getting heavier and heavier, the nightmare monster pulling harder and harder.

"I'm slipping!" his mum yelled.

"NO!" he cried.

He fell forward onto his chest from the weight of her and the nightmare's fists pulling on her.

She screamed again.

And again.

And she was so *heavy,* impossibly so.

"Please," Conor whispered to himself. *"Please."*

And here, he heard the yew tree say behind him, *is the fourth tale.*

"Shut up!" Conor shouted. *"Help* me!"

Here is the truth of Conor O'Malley.

And his mother was screaming.

And she was slipping.

It was so hard to hold on to her.

It is now or never, the yew tree said. *You must speak the truth.*

"No!" Conor said, his voice breaking.

*You **must**.*

"No!" Conor said again, looking down into his mother's face—

As the truth came all of a sudden—

As the nightmare reached its most perfect moment—

"No!" Conor screamed one more time—

And his mother fell.

THE REST OF
THE FOURTH TALE

This was the moment when he usually woke up. When she fell, screaming, out of his grasp, into the abyss, taken by the nightmare, lost forever, this was where he usually sat up in his bed, covered in sweat, his heart beating so fast he thought he might die.

But he didn't wake up.

The nightmare still surrounded him. The yew tree still stood behind him.

The tale is not yet told, it said.

"Take me out of here," Conor said, getting shakily to his feet. "I need to see my mum."

She is no longer here, Conor, his original monster said. *You let her go.*

"This is just a nightmare," Conor said, panting hard. "This isn't the truth."

It is the truth, said the monster. *You know it is. You let her go.*

"She fell," Conor said. "I couldn't hold on to her anymore. She got so *heavy.*"

And so you let her go.

"She *fell!*" Conor said, his voice rising, almost in desperation. The filth and ash that had taken his mum was returning up the cliff face in tendrils of smoke, smoke that he couldn't help but breathe in. It entered his mouth and his nose like air, filling him up, choking him. He had to fight to even breathe.

You let her go, said the monster.

"I didn't let her go!" Conor shouted, his voice cracking. "She fell!"

You must tell the truth or you will never leave this nightmare, the monster said, looming dangerously over him now, its voice scarier than Conor had ever heard it. *You will be trapped here alone for the rest of your life.*

"Please let me go!" Conor yelled, trying to back away. He called out in terror when he saw that the tendrils of the nightmare had wrapped themselves around his legs. They tripped him to the ground and started wrapping themselves around his arms, too. "Help me!"

Speak the truth! the monster said, its voice stern and terrifying now. *Speak the truth or stay here forever.*

"What truth?" Conor yelled, desperately fighting the tendrils. "I don't know what you mean!"

The monster's face suddenly surged out of the blackness, inches away from Conor's.

You do know, it said, low and threatening.

And there was a sudden quiet.

Because, yes, Conor knew.

He had always known.

The truth.

The real truth. The truth from the nightmare.

"No," he said, quietly, as the blackness started wrapping itself around his neck. "No, I can't."

You must.

"I *can't,*" Conor said again.

You can, said the monster, and there was a change in its voice. A note of something.

Of kindness.

Conor's eyes were filling now. Tears were tumbling down his cheeks and he couldn't stop them, couldn't even wipe them away because the nightmare's tendrils were binding him now, had nearly taken him over completely.

"Please don't make me," Conor said. "Please don't make me say it."

You let her go, the monster said.

Conor shook his head. "Please—"

You let her go, the monster said again.

Conor closed his eyes tightly.

But then he nodded.

You could have held on for longer, the monster said, *but you let her fall. You loosened your grip and let the nightmare take her.*

Conor nodded again, his face scrunched up with pain and weeping.

You wanted her to fall.

"No," Conor said through thick tears.

You wanted her to go.

"*No!*"

*You must speak the truth and you must speak it **now**, Conor O'Malley. Say it. You must.*

Conor shook his head again, his mouth clamped shut tight, but he could feel a burning in his chest, like a fire someone had lit there, a miniature sun, blazing away and burning him from the inside.

"It'll kill me if I do," he gasped.

It will kill you if you do not, the monster said. *You must say it.*

"I *can't.*"

You let her go. Why?

The blackness was wrapping itself around Conor's eyes now, plugging his nose and overwhelming his mouth. He was gasping for breath and not getting it. It was suffocating him. It was *killing* him —

Why, Conor? the monster said fiercely. *Tell me WHY! Before it is too late!*

And the fire in Conor's chest suddenly blazed, suddenly burned like it would eat him alive. It was the truth, he knew it was. A moan started in his throat, a moan that rose into a cry and then a loud wordless yell and he opened his mouth and the fire came blazing out, blazing out to consume everything, bursting over the blackness, over the yew tree, too, setting it ablaze along with the rest of the world, burning it back as Conor yelled and yelled and yelled, in pain and grief —

And he spoke the words.

He spoke the truth.

He told the rest of the fourth tale.

"I can't *stand* it anymore!" he cried out as the fire raged around him. "I can't stand knowing that she'll go! I just want it to be over! I want it to be *finished!*"

And then the fire ate the world, wiping away everything, wiping him away with it.

He welcomed it with relief, because it was, at last, the punishment he deserved.

LIFE AFTER DEATH

Conor opened his eyes. He was lying on the grass on the hill above his house.

He was still alive.

Which was the worst thing that could have happened.

"Why didn't it kill me?" he groaned, holding his face in his hands. "I deserve the worst."

Do you? the monster asked, standing above him.

"I've been thinking it for the longest time," Conor said slowly, painfully, struggling to get the words out. "I've known forever she wasn't going to make it, almost from the beginning. She said she was getting better because that's what I wanted to hear. And I believed her. Except I didn't."

No, the monster said.

Conor swallowed, still struggling. "And I started to think how much I wanted it to be *over*. How much I just wanted to stop having to *think* about it. How I couldn't stand the waiting anymore. I couldn't stand how alone it made me feel."

He really began to cry now, more than he thought he'd ever done, more even than when he found out his mum was ill.

And a part of you wished it would just end, said the monster, *even if it meant losing her.*

Conor nodded, barely able to speak.

And the nightmare began. The nightmare that always ended with—

"I let her go," Conor choked out. "I could have held on but I let her go."

And that, the monster said, *is the truth.*

"I didn't *mean* it, though!" Conor said, his voice rising. "I didn't mean to let her go! And now it's for real! Now she's going to die and it's my fault!"

And that, the monster said, *is not the truth at all.*

Conor's grief was a physical thing, gripping him like a clamp, clenching him tight as a muscle. He could barely breathe from the sheer *effort* of it, and he sank to the ground again, wishing it would just take him, once and for all.

He faintly felt the huge hands of the monster pick him up, forming a little nest to hold him. He was only vaguely aware of the leaves and branches twisting around him, softening and widening to let him lie back.

"It's my fault," Conor said. "I let her go. It's my fault."

It is not your fault, the monster said, its voice floating in the air around him like a breeze.

"It *is*."

You were merely wishing for the end of pain, the monster said. *Your **own** pain. An end to how it isolated you. It is the most human wish of all.*

"I didn't mean it," Conor said.

You did, the monster said, *but you also did not.*

Conor sniffed and looked up to its face, which was as big as a wall in front of him. "How can both be true?"

Because humans are complicated beasts, the monster said. *How can a queen be both a good witch and a bad witch? How can a prince be a murderer and a saviour? How can an apothecary be evil-tempered but right-thinking? How can a parson be wrong-thinking but good-hearted? How can invisible men make themselves more lonely by being seen?*

"I don't know," Conor shrugged, exhausted. "Your stories never made any sense to me."

*The answer is that it does not matter what you **think**,* the monster said, *because your mind will contradict itself a hundred times each day. You wanted her to go at the same time you were desperate for me to save her. Your mind will believe comforting lies while also knowing the painful truths that make those lies necessary. And your mind will punish you for believing both.*

"But how do you fight it?" Conor asked, his voice rough. "How do you fight all the different stuff inside?"

By speaking the truth, the monster said. *As you spoke it just now.*

Conor thought again of his mother's hands, of the grip as he let go –

Stop this, Conor O'Malley, the monster said, gently. *This is why I came walking, to tell you this so that you may heal. You must listen.*

Conor swallowed again. "I'm listening."

You do not write your life with words, the monster said. *You write it with actions. What you think is not important. It is only important what you* ***do***.

There was a long silence as Conor re-caught his breath.

"So what do I do?" he finally asked.

You do what you did just now, the monster said. *You speak the truth.*

"That's it?"

You think it is easy? The monster raised two enormous eyebrows. *You were willing to die rather than speak it.*

Conor looked down at his hands, finally unclenching them. "Because what I thought was so *wrong*."

It was not wrong, the monster said, *It was only a thought, one of a million. It was not an action.*

Conor let out a long, long breath, still thick.

But he wasn't choking. The nightmare wasn't filling him up, squeezing his chest, dragging him down.

In fact, he didn't feel the nightmare there at all.

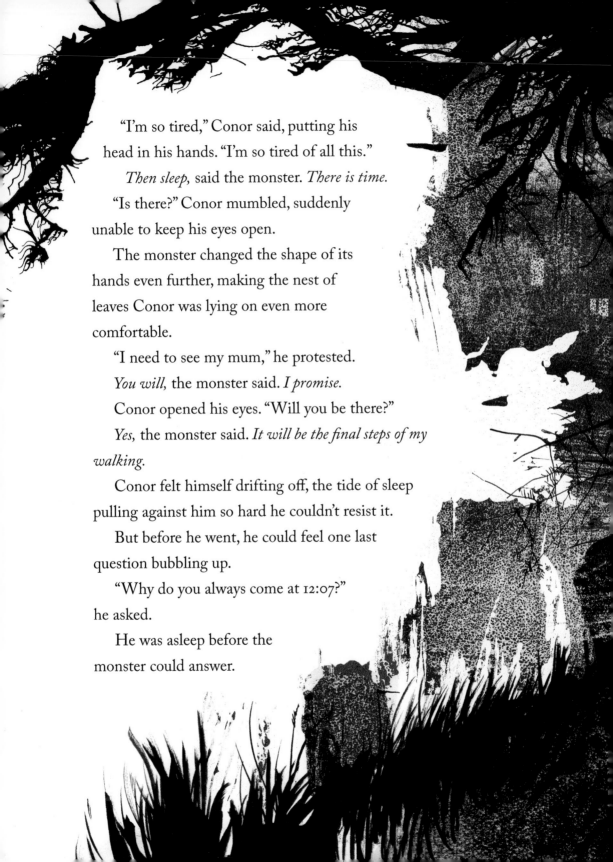

"I'm so tired," Conor said, putting his head in his hands. "I'm so tired of all this."

Then sleep, said the monster. *There is time.*

"Is there?" Conor mumbled, suddenly unable to keep his eyes open.

The monster changed the shape of its hands even further, making the nest of leaves Conor was lying on even more comfortable.

"I need to see my mum," he protested.

You will, the monster said. *I promise.*

Conor opened his eyes. "Will you be there?"

Yes, the monster said. *It will be the final steps of my walking.*

Conor felt himself drifting off, the tide of sleep pulling against him so hard he couldn't resist it.

But before he went, he could feel one last question bubbling up.

"Why do you always come at 12:07?" he asked.

He was asleep before the monster could answer.

SOMETHING IN COMMON

"Oh, thank God!"

The words filtered in before Conor was even properly awake.

"Conor!" he heard, and then stronger. *"Conor!"*

His grandma's voice.

He opened his eyes, sitting up slowly. Night had fallen. How long had he been asleep? He looked around. He was still on the hill behind his house, nestled in the roots of the yew tree towering over him. He looked up. It was just a tree.

But he could swear that it also wasn't.

"CONOR!"

His grandma was running from the direction of the church, and he could see her car parked on the road beyond, its lights on, its engine running. He stood as she ran to him, her face filled with annoyance and relief and something he recognized with a sinking stomach.

"Oh, thank God, thank GOD!" she shouted as she reached him.

And then she did a surprising thing.

She grabbed him in a hug so hard they both nearly fell over. Only Conor catching them on the tree trunk stopped them. Then she let him go and *really* started shouting.

"Where have you BEEN?!" she practically screamed. "I've been searching for HOURS! I've been FRANTIC, Conor! WHAT THE HELL WERE YOU THINKING?"

"There was something I needed to do," Conor said, but she was already pulling on his arm.

"No time," she said. "We have to go! We have to go *now!*"

She let go of him and actually *sprinted* back to her car, which was such a troubling thing to see that Conor ran after her almost automatically, jumping in the passenger side and not even getting the door closed before she drove off with a screech of tires.

He didn't dare ask why they were hurrying.

"Conor," his grandma said as the car raced down the road at alarming speed. It was only when he looked at her that he saw how much she was crying. Shaking, too. "Conor, you just can't . . ." She shook some more, then he saw her grip the steering wheel even harder.

"Grandma—" he started to say.

"Don't," she said. "Just don't."

They drove in silence for a while, sailing through stop signs with barely a look. Conor rechecked his seatbelt.

"Grandma?" Conor asked, bracing himself as they flew over a bump.

She kept speeding on.

"I'm sorry," he said, quietly.

She laughed at this, a sad, thick laugh. She shook her head. "It doesn't matter," she said. "It doesn't matter."

"It doesn't?"

"Of *course* it doesn't," she said, and she started to cry again. But she wasn't the kind of grandma who was going to let crying get in the way of her talking. "You know, Conor?" she said. "You and me? Not the most natural fit, are we?"

"No," Conor said. "I guess not."

"I guess not either." She tore around a corner so fast, Conor had to grab on to the door handle to stay upright.

"But we're going to have to learn, you know," she said.

Conor swallowed. "I know."

His grandma made a little sobbing noise. "You do know, don't you?" she said. "Of course you do."

She coughed to clear her throat as she quickly looked both ways at an approaching crossroads before driving right through the red light. Conor wondered how late it was. There was hardly any traffic around.

"But you know what, grandson?" his grandma said. "We have something in common."

"We do?" Conor asked, as the hospital lurched into view down the road.

"Oh, yes," his grandma said, pressing even harder on the accelerator, and he saw that her tears were still coming.

"What's that?" he asked.

She pulled into the first empty spot she saw on the road near the hospital, running her car up onto the curb with a thudding stop.

"Your mum," she said, looking at him full on. "That's what we have in common."

Conor didn't say anything.

But he knew what she meant. His mum was her daughter. And she was the most important person either of them knew. That was a lot to have in common.

It was certainly a place to start.

His grandma turned off the engine and opened her door. "We have to hurry," she said.

THE TRUTH

His grandma burst into his mum's hospital room ahead of him with a terrible question on her face. But there was a nurse inside who answered immediately. "It's okay," she said. "You're in time."

His grandma put her hands to her mouth and let out a cry of relief.

"I see you found him," the nurse said, looking at Conor.

"Yes," was all his grandma said.

Both she and Conor were looking at his mum. The room was mostly dark, just a light on over her bed where she lay. Her eyes were closed, and her breathing sounded like there was a weight on her chest. The nurse left them with her, and his grandma sat down in the chair on the other side of his mum's bed, leaning forward to pick up one of his mum's hands. She held it in her own, kissing it and rocking back and forth.

"Ma?" he heard. It was his own mum talking, her voice so thick and low it was almost impossible to understand.

"I'm here, darling," his grandma said, still holding his mum's hand. "Conor's here, too."

"Is he?" his mum slurred, not opening her eyes.

His grandma looked at him in a way that told him to say something.

"I'm here, Mum," he said.

His mum didn't say anything, just reached out the hand closest to him.

Asking for him to take it.

Take it and not let go.

Here is the end of the tale, the monster said behind him.

"What do I do?" Conor whispered.

He felt the monster place its hands on his shoulders. Somehow they were small enough to feel like they were holding him up.

All you have to do is tell the truth, the monster said.

"I'm afraid to," Conor said. He could see his grandma there in the dim light, leaning over her daughter. He could see his mum's hand, still outstretched, her eyes still closed.

Of course you are afraid, the monster said, pushing him slowly forward. *And yet you will still do it.*

As the monster's hands gently but firmly guided him toward his mum, Conor saw the clock on the wall above her bed. Somehow, it was already 11:46 p.m.

Twenty-one minutes before 12:07.

He wanted to ask the monster what was going to happen then, but he didn't dare.

Because it felt like he knew.

If you speak the truth, the monster whispered in his ear, *you will be able to face whatever comes.*

And so Conor looked back down at his mum, at her outstretched hand. He could feel his throat choking again and his eyes watering.

It wasn't the drowning of the nightmare, though. It was simpler, clearer.

Still just as hard.

He took his mother's hand.

She opened her eyes, briefly, catching him there. Then she closed them again.

But she'd seen him.

And he knew it was here. He knew there really was

no going back. That it was going to happen, whatever he wanted, whatever he felt.

And he also knew he was going to get through it.

It would be terrible. It would be beyond terrible.

But he'd survive.

And it was for this that the monster came. It must have been. Conor had needed it, and his need had somehow called it. And it had come walking. Just for this moment.

"You'll stay?" Conor whispered to the monster, barely able to speak. "You'll stay until . . ."

I will stay, the monster said, its hands still on Conor's shoulders. *Now all you have to do is speak the truth.*

And so Conor did.

He took in a breath.

And, at last, he spoke the final and total truth.

"I don't want you to go," he said, the tears dropping from his eyes, slowly at first, then spilling like a river.

"I know, my love," his mother said in her heavy voice. "I know."

He could feel the monster, holding him up and letting him stand there.

"I don't want you to go," he said again.

And that was all he needed to say.

He leaned forward onto her bed and put his arm around her.

Holding her.

He knew it would come, and soon, maybe even this 12:07. The moment she would slip from his grasp, no matter how tightly he held on.

But not this moment, the monster whispered, still close. *Not just yet.*

Conor held tightly onto his mother.

And by doing so, he could finally let her go.

A MONSTER CALLS

— · —

THE STORY OF THE BOOK

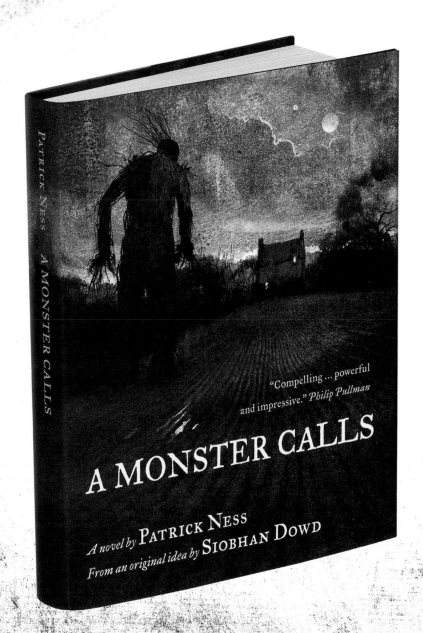

"Compelling ... powerful
and impressive." *Philip Pullman*

A MONSTER CALLS

A novel by PATRICK NESS

From an original idea by SIOBHAN DOWD

WRITING THE BOOK

Patrick Ness, author of A Monster Calls

Patrick Ness

A Monster Calls was meant to be a small project—that's how it was presented to me. I'd just finished the Chaos Walking trilogy, which were all very big books, and was thinking about what I would write next. And then my publisher at Walker Books, Denise Johnstone-Burt, came to me and said, "I've had this idea. Let me know what you think—it can just be something small. Siobhan Dowd had this really lovely idea before she died and maybe we can make something special out of it."

The thing is, though, I didn't want to write a memorial; even for the best of reasons, I don't think a good book gets written that way. It's certainly not what *she* would have written. She would have written a story, and so I was minded to say no. But then there was so much power in what she'd put down that I thought, *Why not give it a try?*

I worked really hard on it and was really pleased with how it came out. And then we brought Jim Kay in and his illustrations were so

The first edition of the book,
published in May 2011 in the U.K.

amazing. And so I thought: *Well, it may have started as just a small thing, but it was something we could all be very proud of. If people responded to it, great, but either way, we'd really all put our hearts and souls into it.*

Then *kaboom!* I had no idea that people would respond in the way they did – I hoped people might, but I never thought they would, certainly not in the way that they have.

My success as a writer has come late, which is good in a way. You always want to have it when you're twenty, but that might not be the best time. I was thirty-nine when *A Monster Calls* was published, and I knew what it was to strive and struggle to work and I really felt how lucky I was to be a part of this. I didn't take any of the awards – the Carnegie Medal and Jim's Kate Greenaway Medal – for granted. I hoped people would respond, and I am just delighted that they did – delighted and amazed that it could have been on this kind of scale.

> *"I hoped people would respond, and I am just delighted that they did."*

I've always felt *A Monster Calls* was never solely a book for children. A good story should be for everyone. A children's book must be for young people first. But if you tell a story that works for a child, it's got to be a good story because children are no fools. I argue constantly for the complexity and validity of the teenage experience because life is lived in the now, not in retrospect. So saying "You'll grow out of it!" may be true, but it's not helpful because you're not living in that grown-up future, and now is just as valid as the future. So Conor's experience is valid because he's experiencing it now, and it's true and powerful because it's happening now.

The journey into adulthood is a journey from innocence into knowledge, but I think it's also a journey from perceived simplicity into complexity. Conor's realization that he can think two contradictory things at the same time—to me, that is a step into adulthood. I think humans are amazing messes, and I love us for our mess. And Conor is just realizing, *Okay, I'm a bit of a mess, but it doesn't make me bad and it doesn't make me wrong. It just makes me human.*

"I think humans are amazing messes, and I love us for our mess."

One of Jim Kay's many early brush sketches for Conor

213

MISTRESS YEW

Denise Johnstone-Burt, publisher and editor at Walker Books

Siobhan Dowd

"The story's theme is healing. It is really my paeon to that great, ancient tree, the yew, without which I might not be alive today, as all the Taxol drugs that so successfully treat breast cancers are derived from it. The yew is the oldest tree in the United Kingdom; it is thought that some live for 2,000 years (and in other parts of the world, yew trees live even longer). The tree is known to be poisonous, especially the red berries on the female variety, but its healing properties were only appreciated in recent decades."
–Siobhan Dowd in an e-mail to Denise Johnstone-Burt, February 2007

A Monster Calls started with Siobhan Dowd in 2003.

I bid for her first published novel, *A Swift Pure Cry,* but I didn't get it; Walker Books came in second in the auction. As part of our pitch for that wonderful young adult novel, we'd designed a beautiful cover, and

Siobhan loved it. She shared our belief at Walker that a book should not only be beautifully told, but also be a special object. So even though I lost the auction, Siobhan and I became friends and she felt she still wanted to publish something with us.

Over the following years, Siobhan and I kept in touch. I e-mailed her late in 2006 and asked her if she "would consider writing a short story—a sort of novella—that we would illustrate and publish." I thought that she was such an outstanding writer that she could write for younger children as well as her teenage audience. I was delighted that Siobhan responded to my request with great enthusiasm. In December 2006 she wrote, "I would hope to write something in the next six to nine months, which would either be a drafty draft, or a more polished opening section, so you could see rapidly if the idea I have got appealed and fitted your vision for this format or not."

It was at this time that Siobhan's condition worsened. Her cancer was terminal but she continued to receive bouts of treatment, working between them and never losing her positive spirit. She e-mailed me in February 2007 and said, "The winter is definitely survivable at this stage. Snowdrops abound and the chaffinches are trilling." In this e-mail she sent me more detail about her idea. She told me she didn't like writing synopses, but with a few deft sentences she gave me a brilliant impression of what she planned: "I haven't a title yet, although it started life as *The Spinney* and I now sometimes think of it as *Mistress Yew*." She went on to talk about the theme of healing and the yew tree—the source of so many drugs against cancer, particularly breast cancer. She mentioned the characters, writing, "In my story there is a boy whose mother is sick and whose life seems lonely." Siobhan also had the idea that the main story would be told through three interwoven stories. "Obviously these stories are linked: what unites them amongst other things is a sense of tree life and human life being interwoven and interdependent."

I was absolutely thrilled with Siobhan's idea and encouraged her to start writing. She began and said she was loving writing it. Then she died, much sooner than we all expected. I was so shocked and saddened by her death—it felt so sudden. Only a few weeks earlier she had made a wonderful speech at the Branford Boase Award ceremony and seemed so vibrant and full of fight.

Some time passed, and Siobhan's agent, Hilary Delamere, contacted me and told me that Siobhan had left a few opening pages to this story. I received the manuscript, about 1,500 words, with great excitement. It was a beginning, and it was presented in such a way that, with her notes, it showed me the characters and how she planned to structure the story. I felt that although it was short, it held real potential. It struck me that it might spark something in somebody else—that there was a really interesting idea here and I shouldn't abandon it.

"It struck me that it might spark something in somebody else."

I talked to Hilary about giving the manuscript to another writer. My immediate reaction was that a woman should take it on. Then one day Patrick Ness was in my office and we were discussing his next book. I suddenly realized what I should do: give it to the best writer I knew. I spoke to him about it and explained about how I wanted to carry on with the project for Siobhan's sake. I wrote to him in December 2009: "I feel that the only way that *Mistress Yew* could come to life is by someone who has a very strong writing voice and who is an outstanding writer which is why I suggested it to you. . . . It seems too special not to do something with, but it could be reimagined in a very different style. I know she was loving writing it. She kept saying she was longing to get back to it."

When Patrick delivered the finished novel some months later, I couldn't believe how brilliantly he had created something entirely his own from Siobhan's fragment. I had always discussed Siobhan's story being illustrated and once I read Patrick's text it seemed right to follow our original plan. We approached the talented Jim Kay and sent him the manuscript. To our great delight he agreed to do a sample, and when we saw his first visuals, I knew we had it.

Ten years later, I feel privileged to have played a small role in the creation of *A Monster Calls* and to have connected two such fine writers in such a special way.

Ink sketch of a yew tree by Jim Kay

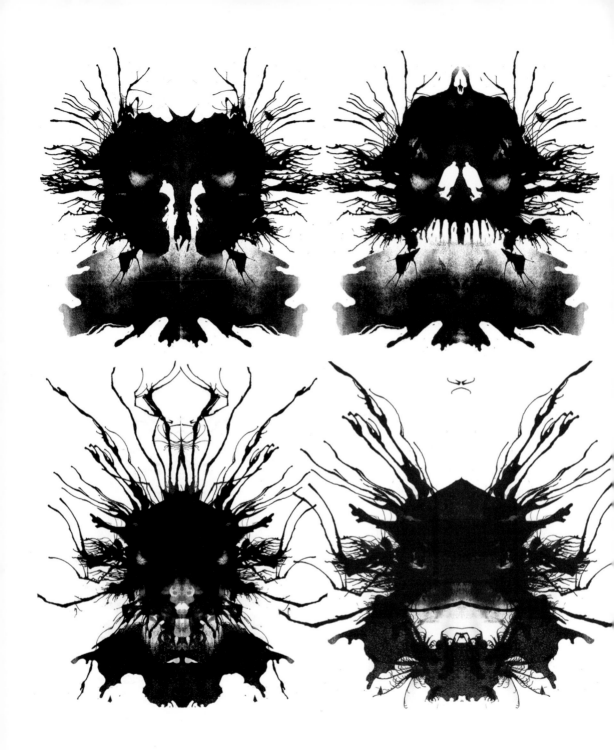

Starting with drips and blown ink marks, Jim Kay assembled these inkblots on the computer. He calls this process "thinking with Photoshop." In these studies, Jim Kay says he first began to get an idea of how the monster might look.

PICTURING A MONSTER

Jim Kay, illustrator of A Monster Calls

I've always loved drawing, but never really thought I could make a living out of it. When I was young I wanted to be an entomologist or a zoologist or anything ending in "gist." I didn't draw for about eight years after leaving university and worked instead in museums and art galleries such as the Tate in London, which at least got me to see a lot of art. But you can't hide from what your heart tells you to do, and ultimately I decided to try illustrating full-time.

Jim Kay

I was very nervous when I was offered the commission to illustrate *A Monster Calls;* the story was so strong, so moving, and I wondered if it should be illustrated at all. But I knew on my first reading (and after sobbing my heart out) that I really wanted to illustrate the book. I had only a weekend to produce a sample – the illustration of the monster leaning up against the house – and was in a state of mild panic, which I think comes across in the image!

When I started the book, art director Ben Norland and I worked on getting the illustrations to flow from page to page in long sequences, and we chose the scenes that might work best. Early on we made a conscious decision, at Patrick's request, to leave the appearance of Conor ambiguous and not to show his face, so as to let the reader keep their own particular vision of the character. Some of the early roughs show my attempts to get closer to Conor in the images, but I left that direction behind.

When work began on the pictures themselves I tried finding all kinds of things to help create the images. I collected hundreds of random marks, smudges, and even my own mistakes. I inked up any objects and materials I could lay my hands on and put them through a printing press. After a couple of weeks, I had amassed a large quantity of paper scraps, each with individual splatters or strange marks on them. I hung these on the walls in my house and began to assemble them into shapes and images. As the days went by, I'd start to see different patterns in them. Some resembled trees, others a hunched figure; in this way I let the images draw themselves to some degree.

Some of the illustrations rely heavily on the impressions made by an old breadboard. The many cuts and

Jim Kay's early sketches were much more literal than the final illustrations

scratches in it produced a wonderful "noise" of delicate marks, which gave the pictures an injection of something extra, an element of something uncontrolled. The texture surrounding the yew sapling growing from the floorboard is a print from the breadboard in reverse. I'll use anything that makes a mark, from quality watercolors to house paints. I like the way cheap materials break up and fail on paper, or poorly-inked linocuts produce strange textures–these are things that can surprise me. I even had a live mealworm beetle on my desk for a while; it stumbled through a spot of ink and left some lovely patterns, which ended up in the book.

The conditions I was working in also affected the illustrations. I was living in a beautiful Georgian apartment in Edinburgh during one of the coldest winters on record. My apartment was usually much colder inside than out, frequently going below zero. I was hardly sleeping–often only four hours a night–and I worked wrapped up in bedclothes. Sometimes my hands were so cold that I couldn't draw anything with fine detail. But in the end that just encouraged me to use big brushes and more energetic printing techniques.

At the time I was also watching a number of black-and-white movies. I'd just been given a copy of the 1922 film *Nosferatu,* and that influenced me. I think in black and white, perhaps because we had a black-and-white TV when I was young. I always think of illustrations as stills from a movie; the fact that the camera can be anywhere and the lighting doesn't have to be direct. And I love setting scenes. I'll start building the props and creating the scenery around the characters. Chairs are lovely to draw, and they relate to human proportions and activities. So an upturned chair is more than just a piece of furniture, it's the echo of a human event.

Sometimes I knew immediately what I wanted in terms of composition, like the monster in the sitting room. But many images were inspired by the different splats and marks I'd been collecting. I'd say 90 percent of them never got past the sketch stage, but usually some element of each failed attempt would creep into the final image.

Illustrating *A Monster Calls* felt like an explosion of relief; finally I had the chance to put some darker, grittier images into a published book. I had been plagued by art directors telling me my work was "too dark" for children, but I know that young people are interested in challenging, sometimes frightening stories—it's convincing adults that's usually the problem.

The illustrations in the book were designed to flow from page to page in long, unbroken sequences.
A reader turning the page might not realize that they are looking at a continuation of the same image.

Conor's house was inspired by memories of the estate in Nottinghamshire where Jim Kay grew up. "I wanted to make a juxtaposition between the ancient, organic monster and the modern, anodyne, and repetitious estate buildings." *—Jim Kay*

The church with its graveyard and yew tree was based on the one in Oxfordshire where Siobhan Dowd is buried.

"These sketches are some of my favorite pieces. Work like this is produced very quickly and unselfconsciously. The challenge is to translate the strength these images have into the final illustrations." *–Jim Kay*

*The industrial landscape is modeled on Pleasley Vale Mill in Nottinghamshire,
which Jim Kay sketched as a schoolboy.*

"In Harrow on the Hill there is a church exactly on top of the hill that has
views right across London. It's a beautiful view. The scene where Conor
falls asleep in the arms of the tree is based on that place." —*Jim Kay*

"I do like this image of Conor in despair and the sense of separation it has, although ultimately it didn't end up in the book. In the final picture all that was left of the composition was the door to Grandma's room." —*Jim Kay*

The image of the destroyed house was influenced by war paintings Jim Kay encountered while working at the Tate's archives in London.

"I wanted the monster to have a real sense of mass and contained power. I feel it has this quality in the image where it sits on the garden shed." *–Jim Kay*

*Jim Kay developed many different ideas for
the monster and explored various directions.*

After Jim Kay had created the book jacket, he turned to the case and endpapers.
"Often illustrators look forward to drawing the endpapers and case that goes under the jacket more than anything else. It's a chance to enjoy pattern and even be a little self-indulgent. There's not the pressure associated with the main illustrations." *–Jim Kay*

During development, the monster took different shapes, some massive, some more angular and spiky. Patrick Ness cautioned about the monster becoming too thin and insect-like. "He was quite right, but you have to try these things out in order to discover that they don't work." –*Jim Kay*

Right: The jacket before the monster's pose and the background had been refined

The final, complete jacket illustration, "unwrapped" from the book

"I have had a recurring dream from childhood of a giant walking through fields, so it was wonderful to be able to illustrate this. There is a kind of visual sequence which begins on the cover with the monster traveling through what is a rural setting, across the title page, through the graveyard, toward the estate, Conor, and the story itself." –*Jim Kay*

cbj, the German publisher of the book, asked for a cover with some subdued color in it that featured Conor, so Jim Kay had the opportunity to develop an entirely new cover approach.

When Jim Kay was developing the image that was to become the new cover image, he was working in Photoshop and accidentally turned on a layer where a bright sun had been moved under the spreading branches of the tree. He immediately recognized the possibility of the tree becoming the monster's head, and the cover concept was born.

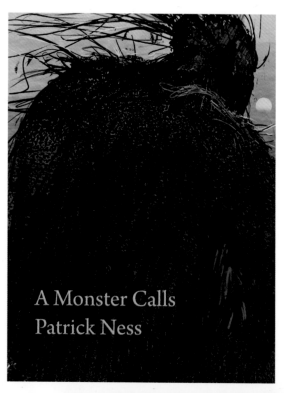

A Monster Calls
Patrick Ness

Right: The final cbj cover

TALKING ABOUT THE BOOK

Julia Eccleshare, a children's book expert and journalist, interviewed Patrick Ness with Denise Johnstone-Burt for Publishers Weekly *to discuss the creation of* A Monster Calls.

What was your thinking about what kind of author you wanted to take it on? Why Patrick Ness?

Johnstone-Burt: I had talked about the idea with a few people. The usual response was that it should be a woman who took it on. Then one day Patrick was in my office and I suddenly realized that the only thing I could do with this was give it to the best writer I knew, so I gave it to Patrick to think about.

Did it feel at all opportunistic? Or exploitative of her name or talent?

Johnstone-Burt: Not at all. The amount of material left was small. Also, I felt that Siobhan would have quite liked the idea. She would have found it interesting and seen it as a way of keeping the story alive beyond the page.

Ness: It wasn't as if it was an undiscovered manuscript draft. She gave it to Denise, and I've seen the e-mails which show that she was fully, fully intending to write it and for it to be her next book.

Can you describe the fragment that you read?

Ness: There was this bit of prose which was small but very full, very vivid, and very potent. It wasn't very polished so to me it felt like a first draft, and that's not an insult. I would never let anyone see my first draft so I felt a writerly sympathy that someone was having a look at it. Then there was the e-mail, which explained that the tree figure would tell three stories for which she said she had great ideas, although she didn't write those ideas down. So it was set up—there was Conor with a name, Lily with a name, and the mother. And the tree coming to life to speak. But it wasn't spelt out what it would say. It was a small piece but packed. It needed a lot of unpacking. Everything was laid out with a great sense of love.

> *"It was a small piece but packed. . . . Everything was laid out with a great sense of love."*

From her notes, could you tell what her ambitions for the story were, and how did you fulfill them?

Ness: She didn't say how she saw it ending. That's the one thing she didn't say. It was a cracking start with a story laid out with great efficiency, which I envy. I really respond to stories within stories, and I thought, "That has an arc. It can really go somewhere." I felt, "This is a writer who's got a story to tell, a great story to tell regardless of impact, regardless of its legacy." It was just that she could feel the story coming together. It was all about to fall into place and she was about to begin. That's why I took it on. It's a thrilling feeling for any writer.

How did you prepare for it? Specifically, did you read all of Siobhan Dowd's books?

Ness: The process of writing it was only a little different, so I prepared like I do for any book. I let the idea stew. I turned it over in my head, usually when I was running because that's what I do. I could see where the story was going. There were a couple of things I decided. There was no way I was going to write it in the voice of Siobhan Dowd. I think those things are terrible. I think they fail because they pay attention to the technical aspects of the story, so I had to have that freedom. I also had to have the freedom to take the story any way I wanted to. That's the same freedom as Siobhan would have given herself. That's what makes a great story. If it grows naturally, if it surprises naturally. That has to happen or the story dies. And if the story dies, then you've written a bad story and that's the worst possible tribute you could pay. So I set aside it being a tribute; I set aside it being in her voice. I just wanted to think about her, writer to writer. Where could I go with her idea? In the end, that was the best tribute.

Johnstone-Burt: I wasn't quite sure how Patrick would take my suggestion when I offered it. I was anxious because it was exposing someone's work. I didn't want him just to finish off the idea. After he had "stewed" we had a really good talk about it and that was when he said the things he's just said. That's when I really took on board that he was writing a completely new book.

What were the challenges?

Ness: There were challenges: at the outset, I could not have been the most obvious choice. There was always the worry that people would say, "What will you do about her voice?" People get very protective after a writer has died, and rightfully so. But, after I'd set aside any expectations—and that's what I have to do with any book—that's very difficult, but vital—I just somehow had to get back to that place like I did when I wrote my first book, which is, No one will probably ever read this book so it can go where it wants to go. Then it became a private conversation between me and her story, her idea. It was a fun place to be even though it was sad. I wanted it to be true. Not hopeless, but true. That's an important part of my writing for teenagers because it was what I wanted as a teenager but rarely got. For me it is really important to have a story with blood in the veins; there are bad tempers and good tempers. It's visceral, physical, and not just one color because that's not how people are.

Once you'd started writing did you feel empowered or restrained by not having had the very first idea?

Ness: It's a paradox. Limitations can be hugely creative and hugely inspiring–so long as they are the ones you choose for yourself. I will not allow anyone to take anything off my palette, but if I do then within that, I can be creative. I viewed it as, "There are limitations because this is the idea but, within that, what can I do? How can I turn it into something?" That's creative and empowering. I had to think, "This is what I've got. How do I spin it?" It's thrilling.

When you read the manuscript of *A Monster Calls* did it make you think of Patrick Ness or Siobhan Dowd?

Johnstone-Burt: Patrick Ness–but I thought Siobhan would love this. She'd be proud of this.

Ness: That's what my goal was. Not to write something she would have written but to write something she would have liked.

Johnstone-Burt: And I think it would have made her laugh.

Did it require much editing?

Johnstone-Burt: No. Not much, but there was some editing, though. In the first draft the monster was visible. I think changing that was a key change.

Ness: I'd argue there was still some ambiguity but yes, it was a change. The story became much more focused on him—on Conor. But I always do make changes. The weave gets tighter and tighter and tighter. The changes were a continuation of the writing.

***A Monster Calls* has been beautifully published [in the U.K.] in an expensive illustrated edition. Was that decision taken to support the concept or was it what you decided once you had read the manuscript and realized the scope of the book?**

Johnstone-Burt: When Patrick agreed to take on the project, I felt I then had to tell the world the terms on which I'd made this deal. And the terms were that it was entirely up to him what he wrote. Whatever it was, we would publish it in the very best way possible.

Ness: I think that's important for all of us. A book cannot apologize for what people may think it should be. It has to be authoritative.

A brush sketch of the monster by Jim Kay

That's what I want as a reader – I want to be confident that the book will do its job. Jim Kay's illustrations are magnificent. Incredible, just fantastic.

A Monster Calls has been extremely well received; your own books have also been very highly praised. Is your response to these accolades the same or is there something special about this book or this idea?

> *"It is something private between me and Siobhan. Something that no one can touch."*

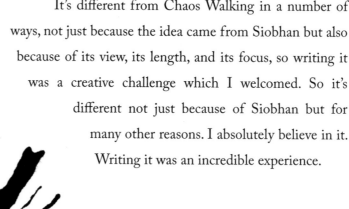

Ness: I don't feel any less or more an owner of this. I feel it's my book in a particular way. It felt like it is something private between me and Siobhan. Something that no one can touch. People can say what they like, but I know how I feel about it and they can't change that. So yes, it does feel like mine. It's different from Chaos Walking in a number of ways, not just because the idea came from Siobhan but also because of its view, its length, and its focus, so writing it was a creative challenge which I welcomed. So it's different not just because of Siobhan but for many other reasons. I absolutely believe in it. Writing it was an incredible experience.

*An early sketch by Jim Kay of the yew tree
in the churchyard behind Conor's house*

A MONSTER CALLS

— · —

THE MAKING OF THE FILM

J.A. BAYONA'S VISION OF
PATRICK NESS'S *A MONSTER CALLS*

J.A. Bayona, director

A Monster Calls is chock-full of layers and psychological riches. One of its main themes is the universally difficult transition from childhood to adulthood, a journey that can never be about a particular or objective age. It's not that you turn thirteen and suddenly morph into an adult. To become another year older is simply to age. To grow up is something altogether different; it is to realize that life is not what you expected or hoped it might be, that it isn't always fair or predictable or controllable. It is to know that sometimes you win and sometimes you lose. Crucially, you understand that you might win and lose at the same time. To truly grow up is to accept the uncertainty.

And growing up can be frightening, all the more so in Conor's circumstances. He is so scared of growing up that when the monster appears Conor isn't frightened of him. In fact, the opposite is true. Conor is so scared of being alone that he doesn't want the monster to leave.

J.A. Bayona and the monster

This complexity reigns in Patrick Ness's novel about a child beginning his life. Far from falling into well-trodden or familiar territory, Conor is one of the most unpredictable, psychologically profound young characters that I have ever had the joy of meeting in any book. His journey to maturity is a rich and confusing one that delves into the darkest nooks and crannies of the young human spirit. Conor's complexity allows for the double pleasure of recognizing yourself in the story while at the same time entering into the unknown.

As if the psychological boldness of the writer weren't enough, *A Monster Calls* also invites and allows us to alternate between the realism of Conor's daily life at home and school, and the world of pure, hard fantasy: monsters, nightmares, princes, and witches march through this dark tale alongside Conor's mother and father, his strict grandmother, his classmates, and a few fearless teachers. Patrick has the capacity to show that fantasy goes beyond the ability to somehow better explain our reality;

Directing the cast and on set with the monster

it can also be the best possible way of articulating our truth.

I believe that *A Monster Calls* is one of those rare novels that will leave its mark forever. The story works on so many levels that everyone who reads it recognizes themselves within it.

At the heart of the book is the power and theme of storytelling. This, above so many other wonderful qualities, is my favorite thing about it. Just as the monster says in the book: "Stories are wild creatures. When you let them loose, who knows what havoc they might wreak?" As a filmmaker, this is what I am dedicated to: to call upon disasters; to rise up as a big liar telling false stories, convinced that a good lie is the best way to shine light into dark corners; and to tell of the mysteries that are our own lives.

"The story works on so many levels that everyone who reads it recognizes themselves within it."

I don't want to end without saying that the seed of this book began in the mind of another writer, Siobhan Dowd. She died before she was able to write it, a victim of the same illness that follows Conor's mother in the pages of the story. I believe that this closeness to the narrative, along with Patrick Ness's extraordinary skills as a storyteller, have combined to create Conor and to make us feel his emotion, which is what gives *A Monster Calls* the timeless ability to touch and to move its reader.

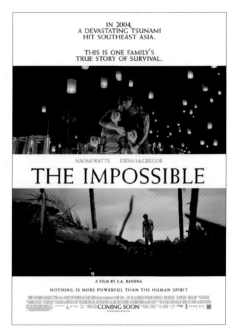

Above: Film posters for J.A. Bayona's previous films, The Impossible *and* The Orphanage
Left: J.A. Bayona on set

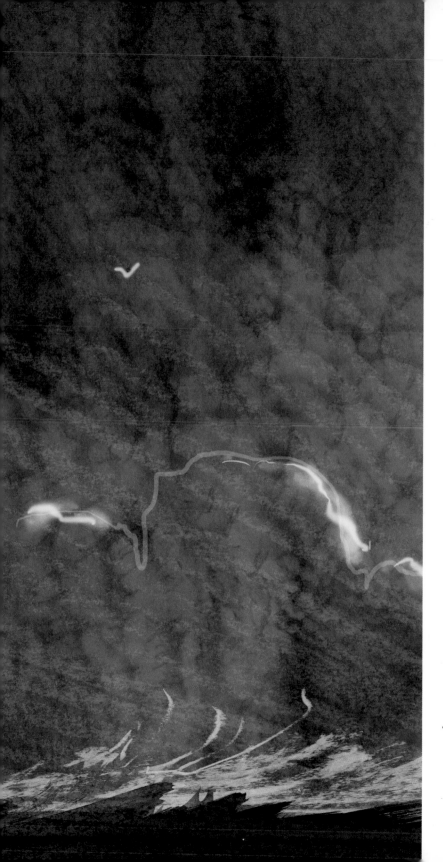

This image was created by Jim Kay for the film.

"Some images were simply for things that I felt I had not fully visually explored in the book." *–Jim Kay*

FROM STORY TO SCREENPLAY

An interview with Patrick Ness

How did you feel when you found out that the book was going to be turned into a film?

Well, it was great, but I am always skeptical. I'm skeptical about everything, even my books–I never believe they're going to exist until they do, and with a film even more so. So much had to be in place that was completely out of my hands. I was optimistic: there were really great creative partners who knew what they were doing and really wanted to make this happen. But I thought, *Movies don't happen to people like me!* So I didn't ever count my chickens–I'm still not counting my chickens!

You have written several screenplays. What was it like adapting your own book into a screenplay? How different a writing experience was it?

I'd been very protective of the material right the way through, so I held off from selling it for a very long time. Then I thought I'd actually like to write the screenplay because I thought I knew how the story works

SOUNDS FADE UP

Nightmare sounds, wind, roaring, screaming.

Sounds increase, climax, then stop suddenly as:

CUT TO:

INT. CONOR'S BEDROOM - NIGHT - CONTINUOUS   1

Conor (12, small, on the border of puberty) sits up in bed,
frightened, sweaty, panting.

He looks at the clock. 11.58.

It's a messy but homey bedroom. Posters at the borders of
manhood on the wall: rugby teams but also cartoons. Old
stuffed toys in corners; framed PHOTOS of Conor and his MUM;
of Conor and friend LILY in a school play; a laptop; handheld
games; scattered DRAWINGS he's made. Conor lays back down to
sleep but:

A heavy COUGHING from offscreen. Conor listens, concerned.
The coughing doesn't come again. He sits up.

INT. CONOR'S HA

Conor pads qui
Mum's bedroom

In the moonlig
is obscured by
sleep.

Conor leaves

INT. CONOR'S   2

Conor is bac
back to slee
in the corne

EXT. CHURCH

A YEW TREE
overlookin
in the moo
branches.
graveyard

Down belo

3B   INT. CONOR'S

                                                            2.

                          ONTINUOUS   3B

and sharpens them. He takes
of a PAPER BAG from an art
through the earlier sketches
, etc, they're very good -

wondering what to draw. His
if on cue:

)

e earth itself. Conor looks
tually hear that?

He looks out his closed
hilltop with the yew tree.
frame on his page for the
ross the desk.

window: the YEW TREE IS

r stands and looks out the
les his hair.

A MONSTER CALLS

Written by

Patrick Ness

Based on the novel "A Monster Calls" by Patrick Ness,
Inspired by an idea from Siobhan Dowd

28 August 2014

Patrick Ness on set with the monster

and how it could be changed so it would work less well. So I wrote it on spec without being paid for it, and to get all the way here just seems incredible. You don't always know that something's going to work; you just hope.

I'll always consider myself a novelist because in a novel, for good or ill, all the choices are yours. You're in charge of it and it's one hundred percent an expression of you. That's a great freedom and a great responsibility and a great challenge—the tyranny of all that choice! It's hard, but really rewarding, and I love it.

Screenplays, on the other hand, are kind of like puzzles: a movie at best is a long short story, so how do you take the essence of your story and communicate everything in it in a shorter space? That kind of creative challenge can spur you on. I've always found limitations can be a great spur to creativity. There's another metaphor I use to describe this: when I was a teenager, I was always trying to work out how I could obey every rule I'd been given to the letter but still get away with what I wanted. Screenplays are a bit like that. The formats are quite strict—the scene, layout and so on—so how do you follow that and give Hollywood all the things it thinks it wants without sacrificing any power and really getting to the punch at the end?

There's so much more input in a screenplay: a movie is so expensive and a lot is riding on it, so lots of people have opinions and you have to try to satisfy everybody, while still being happy with it yourself.

More than a book, a film is a journey from A to B—everything leads somewhere. Luckily *A Monster Calls* is a short book and comes with its own structure, which is naturally leading somewhere: Conor listens to the first story; he steps into the second story; participates in the third story as the invisible man; and the fourth story he tells. So we are going somewhere with him, and that works cinematically. So I thought, *How do I restructure it a little bit to make it fit the shape of a shorter telling, and what tricks can be played filmically to put across ideas that you need several paragraphs to do in prose?*

Because I have my books, I think I am more relaxed when it comes to doing screenplays and more flexible about adapting the novel to suit the screen. I'm still stubborn, but I'm not holding on to everything for dear life and I look at input from the producer and director as a creative opportunity.

What needed to change in the story? How did you feel about altering things from the book? Was there a strand from the book that you wanted to be emphasized in the film?

The bullies get emphasized in the film because they're Conor's connection to the outside world and, given that Conor's world is so interior (he's always in his home, or his grandmother's home, or in the tales), it's important to have this visual link to the outside world in the film. We need to know what the outside looks like, and how the world regards him, and how small his world has shrunk.

There were some changes J.A. Bayona wanted–the director always brings things. He was very interested in the idea of legacy and what a parent leaves behind. So he had the idea that Conor loves drawing because his mother is an artist, and this works perfectly visually because it links right into the tales, which erupt from his drawings. It comes together just gorgeously at the end. Throughout the whole film there's been a locked room in Conor's grandmother's house–it's in that room that she cries when she cries in the book. At the end we discover that the grandmother has been making it into a room for Conor and it's full of his artwork and all his mother's old drawing pads. The final shot shows him opening one up and finding a drawing of the monster on his mother's shoulder, so she has clearly seen the monster herself, probably when she lost her father. So the monster had come for her as well and they share that. It's a beautiful addition: thematically it does just what the book does, but it has visual impact. So there are definitely things that have to change in a film, but you try to retain the spirit of the book.

Were you involved in the casting process for the film? What do the individual actors bring to your characters?

Casting is half desperate desire and half chance. You make lists of actors you want and they're just ridiculous because if you were to get them all, the salaries alone would be $300 million. Liam Neeson is so perfect for the role, it's almost slightly obvious, but we thought, let's try him anyway. And he turned out to love the book, and he's a truly lovely man, so getting him involved felt like a bit of a blessing.

"Liam Neeson is so perfect for the role."

And as for Sigourney Weaver, I don't think we thought she'd be available, but then Bayona called me one day and said, "We've got Sigourney Weaver," and I thought, *Whoa!* And she's perfect— she is physically perfect and her manner is perfect.

Bayona and Belén Atienza [the producer] suggested Felicity Jones and got her before The Theory of Everything—before she was too busy! So that was a great bit of timing. I once talked to a director who said casting is important but, in some ways, if you get good people, the film will sort of shape itself to fit them. But still, how amazing to get Liam

Neeson, Felicity Jones, and Sigourney Weaver for a film that didn't have a huge budget! And among all the kids who were auditioned, Lewis MacDougall just stood out. He's auditioned for three things in his life and he's got all three, so that says it all, really.

Digital concept art for the film

Did you spend much time on set? What did you enjoy most about the filmmaking process?

I was involved in the process all the way through. The director, J.A. Bayona, and the producer, Belén Atienza, were very generous and very collaborative. There were lots of script meetings in Barcelona where we'd talk and talk about scripts, scenes, and order. We hashed it out until we all were happy. I was on set about ten or twelve times. It was a fairly lengthy shoot because they had a juvenile lead, so could only shoot a certain amount of hours a day. Throughout the whole process, they would send me scenes. They would always ask me about additions to the dialogue – every single line of dialogue they were thinking of adding in. Sometimes actors suggest things on set, and some of it's just fantastic and needs to be woven in. Sigourney Weaver had this very funny ad-lib, "He loves it," which is great and really works. So we were sending lines back and forth even after the shooting had finished. The dialogue for the animated tales was also a fun challenge because it had to be a very specific length.

Sets are an incredible combination of absolutely fascinating and completely boring. They're just crushingly dull most of the time, and then when they're not, they're intensely interesting. So I would go to the set in Barcelona and I'd watch for a little while and then I'd go for a nine-mile run and come back and find they'd still be on the same scene!

The first two weeks were spent with Liam Neeson in a suit doing motion capture for the CGI monster. I remember sitting there in the motion-capture studio and they were announcing the second tale in the parson's house, and I was just thinking, *I made this up!* That was amazing. And I learnt a ton. For example, because the monster is created using CGI, they had a big model of the monster's head on set to give Lewis something to act to. And it was so interesting to see how scenes in a car are filmed – they are so high tech, with amazing lighting setups. And the final tale, which is set in a graveyard, was filmed in an abandoned hospital-studio on the outskirts of Barcelona, with a huge construction of a graveyard. It looked half impressive and half not there, but then in the film it looks amazing.

What was it like to work with J.A. Bayona?

It was really fun. The great thing about him is that he isn't proprietary over ideas, so he'd come up with a bunch and if I said, "No and here's why," he'd say, "Okay," and move straight onto the next one. And that lack of ego is so great because it means everyone trusts him and feels free and relaxed enough to suggest ideas. So he just kept coming up with ideas and the producer and I would do the same. We would say exactly what we thought to each other, which is a really good process and you end up with some really great stuff. I have a different cultural background and I was working away in England, so when I came over to Barcelona, I was a useful outside pair of eyes. When I first saw cuts of the film, they had been editing for months and months. I was totally fresh to it, so they were interested in what I saw. I think I had a good function, which I was happy to play.

A Monster Calls is a very emotional novel. How difficult was it to translate the emotion onto the screen?

I think we're a good match, me and Bayona. He's very outwardly emotional and passionate, like a lot of directors are, and I'm very reserved (which doesn't mean unemotional, just privately emotional). So I thought between us we could probably get to a really good central point which neither of us could get to on our own. I would always want to make sure the emotion is really true. I want ugly crying, not pretty crying. I don't want any easy outs (not that Bayona would have gone for easy outs), and he probably instinctively distrusts lack of expression in emotion. So together, we find the right path that most people are going to fall into.

> _"I would always want to make sure the emotion is really true."_

In a movie it's the performances that are going to do it, and all the actors understood that it's not a movie about grief but about sadness and anger. That's an important difference because sadness is cold and anger is hot, but neither is lachrymose. The actors played it with both: they all played it so that they would never fall into an easy sniffle. When I write, I always keep asking myself, Would this really happen? And the actors did this in the film. They really threw themselves into what was hard and raw.

They declined to play it safe or go for what was easy. So you have to give it to the actors; and Lewis, who plays Conor, is such a great actor – there's nothing precocious or stage school about him. It's all real stuff.

Both film and illustration are activities that transform a writer's words into images. What do you feel about that visual process?

I'm not an artist and I'm not a film director, so I felt a huge curiosity about how Jim Kay, the book's illustrator, and Bayona would respond to my work. Jim is so talented! Some of the stuff he drew I could never have thought of, and some of the stuff Bayona shot I could never have thought of. That's what you wish for – somebody who knows different things from what you know and brings those to the work. The important thing for me always is to keep learning. I never want to be complacent – that's why I wanted to do the screenplay myself. Even if I failed, I wanted at least to try. And that's why I've done other screenplays. I want to keep growing, expanding what I can do and finding out new things. Collaborating is part of that.

Has seeing the film changed your perception of the original book?

No, the book is the book. The book stays the book and Jim's drawings stay Jim's drawings.

BEING A MONSTER

An interview with Liam Neeson

What first attracted you to this project?

I was attracted to the project because I was a fan of J.A. Bayona. I saw two amazing films of his – *The Orphanage* and *The Impossible* – which kind of blew me away. When I heard he was doing Patrick Ness's book, *A Monster Calls*, which I had read before, I thought, *That's a marriage made in heaven, right there.*

Do you think there are many differences between the script and the book?

I don't think so. The book is highly imaginative and because we're using motion capture (the technique used to create the monster on set), the film is as rich and imaginative as the book. It's quite a cinematic achievement. The book is essentially magical realism. It's a fable about the complexity of our emotions and navigating that complexity as we're growing up. It's about how to handle loss and death and how to find your place in the world, especially when you're at school. We've all been through that – we all have tales to tell.

"He's the elemental force of the earth, of the universe. He's the wind and he's the sea. He's every animal, every instinct, every emotion that we've ever experienced as human beings. That's who the monster is."

Liam Neeson, Sigourney Weaver, and Ross Mullan at a read-through

Can you tell us about the character you play?

I play the monster, who is conjured up in our young hero's mind. He's huge, like thirty meters tall, and he's made of the earth and ancient trees. The yew tree is his soul. He's kind of like Merlin from the Arthurian legends – he's the elemental force of the earth, of the universe. He's the wind and he's the sea. He's every animal, every instinct, every emotion that we've ever experienced as human beings. That's who the monster is.

What was it like performing using motion capture?

Acting in and with motion capture is a first for me. I hero-worship actors like Andy Serkis, who played Gollum in the *Lord of the Rings* trilogy and Caesar in the *Planet of the Apes* films. I believe those films took months to make; certainly *The Lord of the Rings* took two to three years. In *A Monster Calls* I was involved with motion capture for just two weeks and even that was difficult. You're in a kind of tight wetsuit with little nodules attached that various cameras and computers pick up. They form a skeleton of your shape which is incorporated into the final conception of what the monster will look like.

"While you're acting, you have to be very, very focused and forget about all the technicals."

While you're acting, you have to be very, very focused and forget about all the technicals; otherwise they would just swamp you. You really have to be on top of your game. But I must say, after two

270

or three days I kind of got into the swing of it—you do get into a rhythm. And the motion-capture people we were working with in England were just fantastic. So they made life a lot easier.

What is it like working with children and with Lewis MacDougall especially?

I've worked with quite a few kids over the years. Lewis MacDougall is a very special young boy. I've worked with children who have been overwhelmed by the business, overwhelmed by the industry, and they've lost a kind of childlike innocence, appreciation, and curiosity. But Lewis has got all that intact. He's a real kid and a very powerful young actor. He has a lovely screen presence. He's great fun and very easy to interact with. He's a special boy.

How was working with J.A. Bayona?

Working with J.A. Bayona was wonderful. I'm so lucky. I've done sixty-three, sixty-four films and every so often I've worked with directors who are just steeped in the love of what they do. J.A. is certainly one of those directors. He eats, sleeps, and drinks motion pictures. He's kind of like a walking encyclopedia—

> *"He protects you; he guides you and nurtures you, and he will take as long as it takes to get it right."*

he's a bit like Martin Scorsese in that way. He's also very, very sensitive and he loves his actors. He loves his technical staff, of course. But when everything's all set up for shooting a scene—and it sometimes takes forever with motion capture to get all the cameras right and all the computers ready—J.A. always comes down before he calls "Action!" to talk to the actors about what the scene's about. He protects you; he guides you and nurtures you, and he will take as long as it takes to get it right. I love working with a director like that.

What do you hope the audience will take away from this film?

I think when audiences see this film they're going to be stunned by the technical achievement of the motion capture and how it is integrated into the story. It's a very moving, heartfelt story. There's some comedy in it, but I think audiences will connect with the emotion most of all.

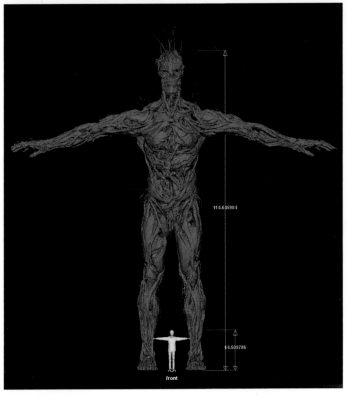

Above: Conor and the monster
Left: Developing the scale
of the monster
Previous spread:
The finished monster

114.645984

44.509786

front

PLAYING CONOR

An interview with Lewis MacDougall

How did you get your role in the film?

Well, it all started from being in the film *Pan* and meeting Ben Perkins, who is my chaperone. He was hired as the acting coach on *A Monster Calls* and he put me forward for the part of Conor. I went to two auditions in London and then a screen test in Barcelona. I was actually on holiday with my dad when I found out I'd got the part. We were just in our room and we got a phone call and I was really excited and I couldn't wait to get started. I hadn't read the book before, but when I read the script I just thought what a good story it was and how much I was looking forward to telling it.

What did you like most about the story?

Conor's relationship with his mother, which I thought was a really nice relationship, and also the scenes with the bullies.

277

Conor faces a bully.

Did you have to do any preparation to play Conor?

Nothing specific, but I have thought about things that have happened in my own life. The film follows the death of Conor's mother, and my mother died a year ago, though it was in different circumstances. I think what Conor struggles with is the fact that nobody in his life is really telling him the truth. He doesn't really have anybody he feels he can turn to, and the monster becomes that person. But in my life, my dad has always told me the truth about my mother's illness.

When did you first meet Liam Neeson, who plays the monster?

I first met Liam at the read-through. Then we went on to do two weeks of motion capture, which was quite difficult because it was so technical. I was standing at one end of the room and he was

Lewis MacDougall acting with the monster

Above: Smashing up Grandma's house; Conor and his dad; The final truth
Previous spread: Conor meets the monster for the first time at 12:07.

standing at the other. I wasn't actually acting to him because he was on the other side of the room, but on camera they made it look like I was standing right in front of him.

What have you learnt from working with Sigourney Weaver, who plays your grandmother, and Felicity Jones and Toby Kebbell, who play your mum and dad?

Well, Sigourney is such an accomplished actress – she taught me a lot. I have one scene with her where she gets in a real state and that taught me how to play off the other actor in a scene. With Toby, we were always having such a laugh because he's a bit like a kid. He taught me that if I don't get something right the first time, not to worry about it, but just do it again. And with Felicity, it was really, really great because we got so close on the shoot. She helped me conquer my fear of roller coasters at the start, and we did so many things together, like we went to the zoo. We also went to the Indian restaurant where we had to be our characters. Everybody around us was staring at us because Jota [J.A. Bayona] and Ben were on the table next to us and they were passing us notes, telling us what to say to each other. It was a really funny moment.

What was it like to work with Jota, the director?

It's great working with Jota. He's always pushing me to do better, and at the end of every scene, he always gives me a hug and says thank you. Working with my acting coach, Ben, was also really fun and, to be honest, I would not have been able to do this whole film without him. I mean, every day he taught me something new, and it's really been a great experience to work with him.

Which scene or moment did you enjoy the most, and which did you find the most challenging?

The bits I enjoyed the most were the scenes with the bullies. Also when I went to the fairground at Blackpool Pleasure Beach with Toby, we were having a hot dog and then a sea gull came and took it and flew away with it! It was sad that we didn't get it on camera. My most challenging scene is quite an obvious one – the nightmare. It was cold and it was wet, and I had to go through a lot of tough emotions and do stunts at the same time.

How was your life during the shoot? What in your life has changed since you started working in films?

During the shoot, it's sometimes been quite difficult. If I've been doing a really emotional scene, having to go straight from that to tutoring and something like maths is hard. In terms of my life outside films, it's definitely changed. I've got more confident and I've got to meet so many really, really cool people. But when I am back home, I sort of play it down a bit, so there I have a normal life really.

UNDERSTANDING GRANDMA

An interview with Sigourney Weaver

Why did you want to be involved with *A Monster Calls*?

Well, I loved the script. It was a very haunting, moving story–
an important story, I thought. And I felt it would be in very
good hands with J.A. Bayona. I think it takes a very unusual

Grandma and Conor in an emotional scene

"*It's a very beautiful, powerful book. I think it has a lot of respect for children and what they experience—what they feel and what they fear.*"

director to find the balance between the two parts of the story in *A Monster Calls:* the grim reality of the mother's illness and the fantasy world that Conor escapes into. I thought Bayona was the perfect person to do it.

Did you know Patrick Ness's novel before you got the script?

No, I didn't know about the novel. When I heard about the project, I ordered it, and it's a remarkable book. I actually sent it to my nieces and nephews because I thought they were old enough. It's not for a little child, but it's a very beautiful, powerful book. I think it has a lot of respect for children and what they experience–what they feel and what they fear. It doesn't pull its punches, but it's also a very loving book with a lot of heart.

What were the highlights of the script and the moments that touched you the most?

I think the relationship between Conor and the monster is so unexpected, especially in the script because there are more jokes. Conor makes fun of the monster and how he never learns anything from him. As for my character–the grandmother–she is rather scary, but her point of view is very relevant.

How did you prepare for your character?

First I worked on the character's voice, which I felt would have a certain formality. There was a lot I could use from my own life: I am a mother, so I know that mothers do try to interfere, even though we don't think we're interfering. At the beginning Conor doesn't really like his grandmother because she's so different from his mother, but I love the growth of their relationship over the course of the story. It was exciting to play someone who really begins in one place and ends in another.

I also had a lot of support in portraying the character physically. The costume designer, Steven Noble, helped and so did my makeup artist. She thought the grandmother should have pink nails because at the start, I am someone who is keeping it all together, but by the end, everything has fallen apart.

Did you research cancer and bereavement when preparing for your role?

I went on a lot of websites and blogs that are about ovarian cancer and family support, and I talked to a couple of friends who've been through it. When we were in Manchester, we had a remarkable visit from an oncologist and a woman from Macmillan Cancer Support, and Felicity Jones and I visited a hospice. I think each of us, in our own way, tried to find out as much as possible about the details of the illness and its

Grandma and Conor in the car

> **"***The scenes are very tough if you have loved ones who've experienced cancer, and all of us do. It was very important to all of us that we got it right.***"**

Exploring the family dynamic

development. We had a fair amount of research between us all and that helped very much.

What was your most challenging scene?

They're all challenging, but the most challenging one was probably the scene where the grandmother and Conor make peace. It's toward the end and we are in a car and it's raining. When we were filming, Jota [J.A. Bayona] did this strange thing where he uses a microphone and directs us from afar, so we couldn't see him. We could only hear him—which was odd because I'm used to a director coming over and whispering in my ear.

I think all of the scenes are very tough if you have loved ones who've experienced cancer, and all of us do. It was very important to all of us that we got it right—that we told the story truthfully, with love and respect—so I think we really tried to put our all into each of the scenes.

What can you say about Lewis MacDougall and his work?

I have so much admiration for Lewis MacDougall. First of all, I think he's very talented. He's also such a good sport—he's working very long hours, he's the lead of the movie, and if he's not in the scene, he's watching whoever is talking. It's a very demanding role physically and emotionally. He's so courageous and also so present. I've really learned a lot about acting from Lewis because he's very much in the moment.

It's been a wonderful experience working with him, and he's just done a fantastic job.

What was it like working with Felicity Jones?

Felicity is such a wonderful actress. I've always admired her work and I think she brings such passion to the role of the mother. Our relationship (in the film) is difficult because she thinks I'm interfering, while I think I'm saving her, so that's all juicy stuff. And I think from the very beginning Felicity and I trusted each other so much – trusted that we could have a huge fight on camera and bring as much reality to it as possible.

How was working with J.A. Bayona?

He tells the story in a very different way from how most directors would. I also think he's the perfect director for this film because he's so good with young actors. He also cares so much about the material and has this really strong vision of the reality of the family on the one hand and the fantasy of the monster on the other. It's challenging to balance those different worlds and I felt like he was constantly weighing it up.

What do you think the audience is going to find in the film?

I think the audience will be taken on a journey, just as the boy is. It's a big adventure, but there's also a lot of humor in the script, thank goodness. The trick, I think, is to keep taking the audience in and out of this very powerful material, so they have enough energy to go with us to the end.

Do you have a memory of the shoot you would like to share?

Well, one interesting, very unusual thing that happened was this: we had a series of scenes where the family's together. They're not easy scenes—there are a lot of disagreements

J.A. Bayona directing on set

leading up to one big disagreement. In the end, before we shot the big disagreement, which was one of our most difficult scenes and not in the book, Jota ran through it all in his mind and said, "You know, we don't need that scene. We have accomplished what we need with the earlier scenes and we've got enough. We don't need to shoot the final enormous fight." And I was so filled with admiration for that because most directors shoot everything just to make sure, and he had the confidence and the understanding of the story to say that we didn't need to do it. I can't say that's ever happened to me before—usually you just shoot everything and half of it ends up on the cutting-room floor.

REVEALING A MOTHER'S LOVE

An interview with Felicity Jones

What attracted you to the project?

I was a big fan of J.A. Bayona and his work: the way in *The Impossible* he uses the tropes of horror to tell the story of the 2004 tsunami. I also liked his episodes of the TV series *Penny Dreadful*. So it started with him. I hadn't read the book before, but obviously, having read the script, I went straight to the book and loved it. It seems so simple on the surface, but what you see through the boy's eyes, or beyond the boy's eyes, are actually very complicated human relationships and interactions.

When you first read the script, what moments touched you the most?

I loved the moments when the boy is talking to the monster. I loved the way the monster isn't too cuddly and that there's an antagonism between Conor and the monster. It's hard for Conor because the monster is teaching him lessons that are incredibly difficult to grasp. The story is about life and love, and in many ways it's about two people

Felicity Jones as Conor's mother, Lizzie

trying to let go of each other – two people who have the most profound love for one another. It's about what everyone has to go through growing up. It's about how things don't always work out, but how you can find strength through those difficulties.

Tell us about your character and her situation.

Well, we first encounter Lizzie, Conor's mother, in the screenplay when

Mother and son share a happy moment.

she's going through her second round of cancer. She's already had ovarian cancer and it's come back. Lizzie has a very artistic spirit: she loves drawing and making little films. She's always documented her and Conor's life together, so we see flashbacks, through her films, to a time earlier in her life when she was healthier. She's a single parent and there's an incredible bond between her and Conor—there's a sense that they're not only mother and son, but they're also friends. There's an incredible closeness between them.

Felicity Jones in hair and makeup

How did you prepare for the role?

Cancer affects millions and millions of people, so playing the role of a woman suffering from cancer was something that I felt instinctively I wanted to get right. I approached it very academically at first and found out about the disease and how it manifests physically. I visited oncologists because I wanted to get the medical perspective–to know exactly what drugs you have to take, to know how people try to fight the disease. It was also incredible speaking to people who were going through chemotherapy–women who were very frank about their experiences and the daily rituals they use to cope.

During the filming, I worked with an amazing team of experts in prosthetics in order to show how the cancer is affecting Lizzie's body, and I also lost weight. I wanted to show how her breathing changes and her body weakens. When I looked at the script, it felt like there were four specific changes in her physicality that we needed to show, and it was about trying to show those shifts as subtly as possible but also as truthfully as possible.

What was the most difficult scene emotionally?

What's so difficult for Lizzie and Conor is admitting to each other that she is going to die. They don't want to say it to each other because understandably they don't want to lose each other – they can't imagine a world without each other. So there was a particular scene when Lizzie finally has to admit to Conor that she's very, very sick and it doesn't look good, and that was extremely difficult. But she is a vibrant and active woman who loves art and being a mother. The film is very much a celebration of living and appreciating life.

"They can't imagine a world without each other."

On set with Sigourney Weaver and Lewis MacDougall

What was it like working with Lewis MacDougall?

Well, Lewis MacDougall is just phenomenal. You can't reduce him to words (even though I'm now going to try to do that!). He's such a professional actor. He takes it very seriously, and he cares immensely about the story and about getting the character right. But he's also playful. He has this amazing ability to be on camera and be completely unfiltered and honest. He's intelligent and just lovely to work with.

Tell us about your character's relationship with her mother, who is played by Sigourney Weaver.

> *"There's enormous love between this mother and daughter, but there are also complications."*

In many ways Lizzie is a bit of a rebel. She had Conor when she was very young. She fell very much in love with his father at the time, but the relationship has since broken down. So she's impulsive, and sometimes that's difficult for her mother and there's a bit of friction between them. In some senses, Lizzie wants Conor to be free, to be independent, to smash things up when he's angry, because she's never quite been able to find her own freedom from her mother. Sigourney and I wanted to show that there's enormous love between this mother and daughter, but there are also complications.

Sigourney is someone I hugely respect as an actor. I've learned so

Previous spread: The final scene with the monster at 12:07

much from her, and it's been wonderful to speak to her about working in film as a woman. She's been a mentor in many ways. She's just so extraordinary to watch on-screen—she always brings such depth to her work. And she bought me a lovely all-in-one fleecy suit, which is the best Christmas present anyone could ever get!

Some of the filming was done in Spain. Was it odd filming such a U.K.-based story in Barcelona?

Not at all, but I'm just overawed by the sets because there's not a single item or dressing or doorway that doesn't look entirely English. The design has very much captured a sense of northern England. Lizzie doesn't have a lot of money, and they're not a wealthy or materialistic family in any way. It's lovely to see how all of those nuances are expressed in the sets.

Is it true that Bayona plays music to get the actors in the mood before a scene?

Yes. He tries to make it as easy as possible for you to find the emotional depth of the scene or the character, so he plays music to create the mood. We were doing one scene where we had to be upbeat, so we were listening to Nicki Minaj before we started. Lewis is a big fan of Nicki Minaj. It's wonderful having that blaring out on speakers before you do a scene—it helps get rid of your self-consciousness.

Do you have a memorable moment from filming you'd like to share?

Too many! We did a fantastic scene where Lewis and I were both attached to abseiling ropes. It was the nightmare scene when Lizzie falls and the floor is opening and Conor runs to get her and tries to hold on to her. It was quite fun doing an action sequence, being suspended from ropes in a harness, like a big baby! Another moment was when we went to the swimming pool and Lewis and I were splashing around and filming each other on this little GoPro camera. It's been wonderful to go from doing little intimate scenes like that to the much bigger operatic scenes, like the one when Lizzie dies at the end of the film.

Left and above: Rehearsing and working on the nightmare scene
Next spread: Illustration for the film by Jim Kay showing Conor's nightmare

CONOR'S SKETCHBOOK

Developing the character's artistic vision

One theme director J.A. Bayona explores in *A Monster Calls* is the idea of legacy and what a parent leaves behind for a child. Lizzie, Conor's mother, is an artist and she has inspired a love of drawing in Conor as well. We see Conor with his sketchbook frequently in the film. His drawings become a way for him to express his inner emotional turmoil–both the fear of being left alone and the fear of letting his mother go. Conor's drawings also help link his everyday world to the animated fantasy world of the monster's tales. Visually the tales appear to come straight out of his sketchbook, creating a link between the different parts of the story.

Conor's drawings also become a way to explore the universality of human experience. Throughout the film we see a locked room in Conor's grandmother's house. At the very end, we find out that Conor's grandmother has been turning it into Conor's room, filling it with his works of art and his mother's old sketch pads. The final shot of the film shows him opening one and finding a drawing of the monster on his mother's shoulder. So Conor is not the only person to have seen it; the monster has come for her, too. It's a powerful moment. By the end of the film, even though his mother is no longer with him, this shared experience makes her and Conor closer than ever before.

Previous page: Conor drawing at Grandma's house
This page and right: Inside Conor's sketchbook

Digital concept art created for the development of the monster

RAISING THE MONSTER

From ancient tree to CGI creation

Jim Kay's original pen-and-ink vision of the monster inspired the breath-takingly real CGI creation in the film. Hoping to understand more about this strange and elemental being, J.A. Bayona approached the illustrator and asked him to develop his original drawings of the monster, wanting to see exactly how it was made. Kay admits he has always been fascinated by the relationship between the monster and the yew tree, and in the drawings he did for Bayona the roots and branches of the yew tree sinuously entwine, creating the monster's form.

From Kay's drawings of the monster came the concept art for the CGI. While remaining true to Kay's original vision, the concept art explored the monster's character further. The art looked at the physicality and energy of the monster, and the process by which the tree transforms into the monster's form. From there, through graphics and models, came the finished CGI: a twisting mass of roots and branches with glowing eyes – a true force of nature.

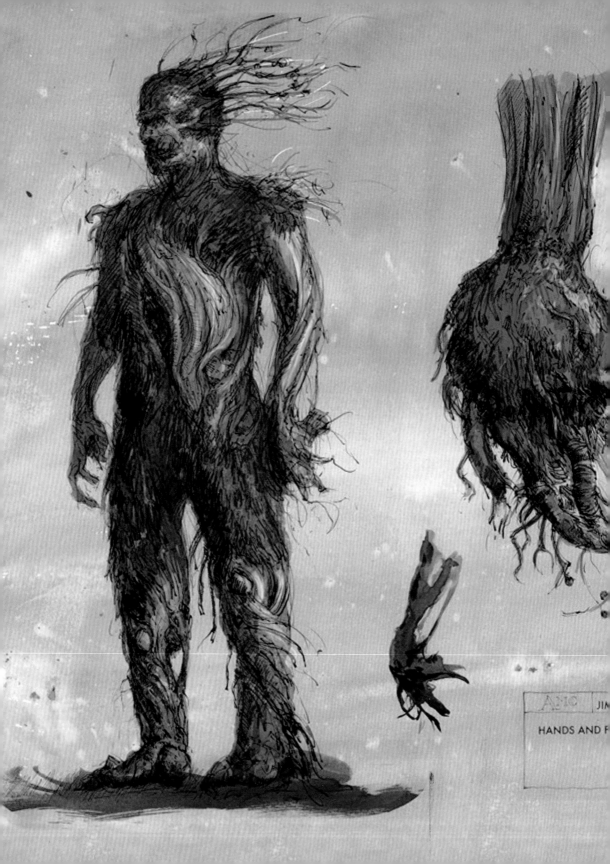

A110   JIM

HANDS AND F

*Concept illustrations for
the film by Jim Kay*

"Bayona gave me no brief
for the new drawings
of the monster. He just
asked me to produce more
images and to show more
of what it looked like.
This is tricky territory for
an illustrator, because in a
book you can deliberately
avoid showing too much
or going into the details
of how the creature
is made." *–Jim Kay*

Concept art by Jim Kay. The anatomy of the monster is based on photographs he took of the root systems of trees, exposed after storms had felled them.

"I like the idea that the roots and branches form the monster's tendons and muscles, and that the leaves make up his flesh. But also bits of mud and rock can get trapped within the monster and form things like his ankle or the ball of the foot. Yew trees have the most amazing roots."

—Jim Kay

*Digital concept art showing the
transformation from yew tree to monster*

Above and bottom right: Developing the monster's facial expressions
Top right: Concept art for Conor's nightmare

This page: Modeling the monster
Right page: The finished monster

"I WILL TELL YOU THREE STORIES"

Adrian Garcia, creative director at Headless,
the company that animated the monster's
tales, tells the animators' tale

We knew that this would be a challenging project. However, the richness of the source material and the fact that we'd be working with such a prestigious filmmaker gave us the confidence to take on the project without any hesitation.

Our challenge was to make the tales fit with the rest of the film. We didn't want them to feel whimsical, so we went for something artistic and hand-drawn that would link to Conor's imagination and his creative spirit. With that idea in mind, the designs contained graphic elements inspired by his drawings, including the broken strokes and the inkblots. We generated the bases of the scenes with 3-D software and added the handmade elements later to create the hand-drawn look of the image. Each shot presented challenges and there were different solutions for each one.

Furthermore, the animation needed a certain degree of cinematic complexity to avoid breaking the narrative pace of the film. It was very complicated for the animators to make the

naïf element of the drawings fit with the tone of the piece. We wanted the images to define the technique, not the other way around.

We created a deliberate evolution in the style of animation for each tale, starting with the more abstract and stark first tale, where the images grew from an inkblot. In the second tale we used a more defined physical and spatial reality, with a more painterly treatment reminiscent of an oil painting by the end of the tale. This becomes the world that envelops Conor and the link between both realities.

Collaborating with J.A. Bayona pushed us to work organically and adapt our methods, so all the parts of the film grew together and nurtured one another.

This page and left: Concept art for the animations

*Above and left: Stills and concept art from
the animation of the first tale, showing
the prince and the farmer's daughter
Below: Concept art by Jim Kay*

Above and left: Concept art and stills from the animation for the second tale
Next spread: The monster destroys the Apothecary's house.

CREATING CONOR'S WORLD

An interview with production designer Eugenio Caballero

How did you end up working on the film?

I had worked with J.A. Bayona on *The Impossible*, which was a fantastic experience for all of us. There's a lot of freedom when you work with him. We talk a lot about concepts. I trust him and we trust each other, and for me that's a very important thing.

The possibility of working with the same group of people – the same producers – was an added bonus. I also read the book and saw lots of potential to work together with the crew to make both an interesting film and a film that would really challenge me.

Were you inspired by Jim Kay's illustrations in the book?

You cannot read the book without being aware of those beautiful illustrations. They were a starting point, a reference to which we could turn. They brought some light to some of the obscure parts of the creative process. We honored them in that way.

Filming the final scenes with the yew tree in the churchyard

How did you design the houses where Conor's mother and grand-mother live?

For me, designing for films is a narrative discipline. The spaces I design have to reflect what is happening with the characters and what is happening in the story at that moment. The mother's house and the grandmother's house are the two big interiors in the film. The mother's house – Conor's house – is way messier and it has a much warmer atmosphere. The grandmother's house is much more severe. Everything is in a very strict order and every single item has its position, so it's very off-putting for a boy who is used to living in a house of freedom.

We tried to accentuate the desperate feeling that Conor experiences when he has to go and stay with his grandmother. We made the set of her house a little bit bigger than it would normally be, so the character of Conor would look smaller. We used dull colors to contrast with the more colorful, joyful palette in Conor's house. I also used lots of straight lines and angles in the grandmother's house, which create a feeling of hostility. In Conor's house everything is rounded, and the mood is embracing. One of the main ideas in this film is that the fantasy is created from the boy's need to have hope, despite his despair. In my designs I wanted there to be a link between the reality and the fantasy, so there are elements of the fantasy world planted in the mother's house.

Top left: Grandma's house
Bottom left: Lizzie and Conor's kitchen

Do you like fairy tales? Were you influenced by them for these sets?

I do like fairy tales and I think they have a lot of relevance to our film. For example, there are lots of stories within the main plot. Also the landscape in Manchester, where we shot several key scenes, with all the mills, red brick, chimneys and Victorian architecture, reminds me of those tales illustrated by Arthur Rackham and Edmund Dulac – the classic illustrators of Victorian fairy tales. They were definitely in the back of my head when we started developing this film.

How closely do you work with the special effects teams to find the look for the film?

I work closely with them. What we started to do in *The Impossible,* and are trying to do in this film, is to mix new high-tech capabilities, visual effects, motion-capture techniques, and 3-D printing with very traditional techniques. I used molds and plaster, which are very traditional techniques, with very modern techniques. I think it's a great combination and works well.

From the top: Concept art; digital art; the final churchyard gates

Above and right: Creating then destroying the church in the nightmare scene
Next spread: The set for the churchyard

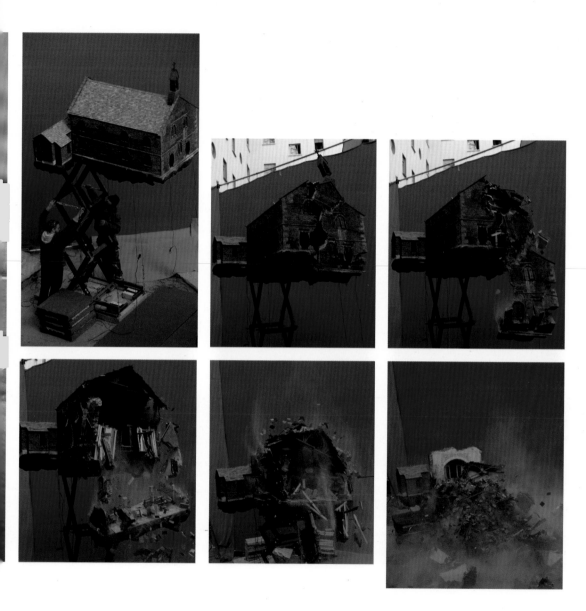

An interview with
costume designer Steven Noble

How much were you influenced by current fashions when designing the costumes?

A design for one of Grandma's costumes

I deliberately didn't follow current fashions, and there were several reasons for that. The first was that it would be a while before the film would be released and I didn't want the costumes to look dated. Second, I thought the characterization needed some sort of slightly otherworldly aspect to it. Conor and his mum needed to look a bit eccentric. I sourced all the pieces in London and Manchester. There are some that we bought new and I've tried to mix them together with secondhand things, some things that I've made, and Conor's hand-knitted sweaters.

How did you decide on the look of the costumes?

It was a four-way conversation between the character, the actor, the director, and myself as to where we saw that character going and what they should look like. Obviously the actor is playing a character, so you try not to incorporate too much of their personality within the costumes of the character they're playing. But then again the actor will always bring a little bit of himself or herself to that character, so it's a balance.

> *"It was a four-way conversation between the character, the actor, the director, and myself."*

What do you think the audience will find in *A Monster Calls*?

I think *A Monster Calls* is a modern-day fairy tale. I think it's an important book and I think it's an important film. I work with a commercials producer who's a single mother with a young boy. I told her that I was working on this and she went, "Oh, my God! That's my son's and my favorite book." And then she elaborated by saying that he was having problems at school and being bullied. They read the book together and it opened up so many conversations that she thought that they'd never be able to have. I think that sums up how important this film is.

Lizzie's costume

First U.S special collectors' edition 2016

Library of Congress Catalog Card Number 2010040741

ISBN 978-0-7636-5559-4 (original hardcover)
ISBN 978-0-7636-6065-9 (original paperback)
ISBN 978-0-7636-9238-4 (special collectors' edition)

16 17 18 19 20 21 GCR 10 9 8 7 6 5 4 3 2 1

Printed in Bucharest, Romania

This book was typeset in Adobe Caslon Pro.

Candlewick Press
99 Dover Street
Somerville, Massachusetts 02144

visit us at www.candlewick.com

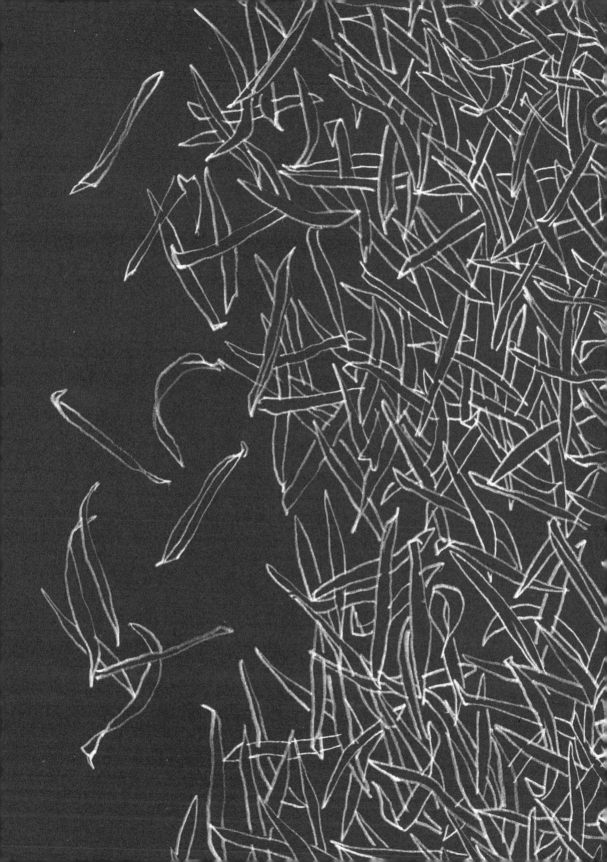

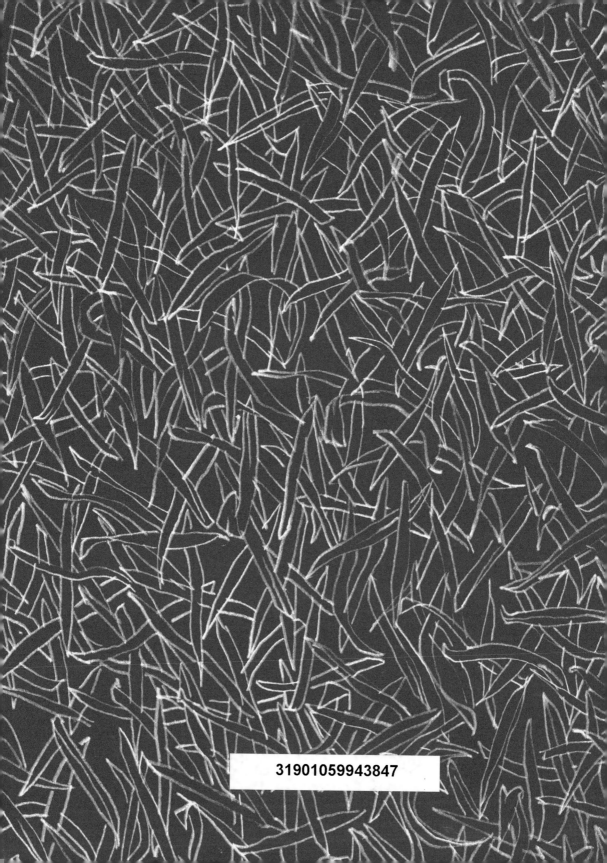

31901059943847